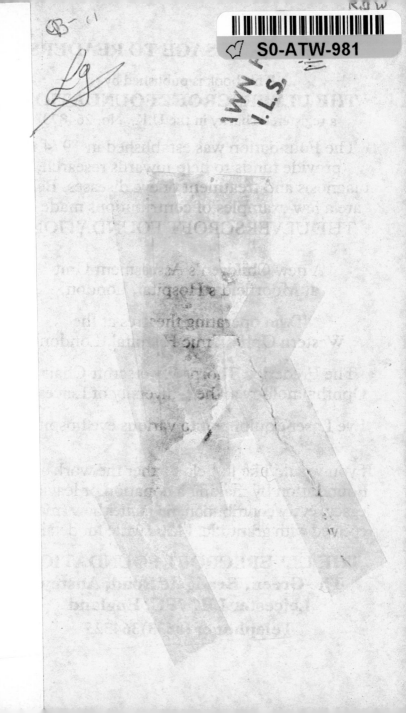

BODIE: HIGH HELL

Angela Crown wanted to hire Bodie's gun. It wasn't Bodie's usual line of work, but something about Miss Crown convinced the Stalker that the job would be worthwhile. He was set against a ruthless landowner who wanted Angela Crown's mine and wasn't to let one gunman stop him getting it. That was just one of the bounty hunter's problems. There was also a beautiful, wealthy and cold-blooded whore called Beth Arling and she, too, had good reason to want Bodie dead . . .

NEIL HUNTER

◆

BODIE:
HIGH HELL

Complete and Unabridged

LINFORD
Leicester

First published in Great Britain in 1979

First Linford Edition
published February 1994

British Library CIP Data

Hunter, Neil
Bodie the stalker no.3: high hell.
—Large print ed.—
Linford western library
I. Title II. Series
823.914 [F]

ISBN 0–7089–7495–3

Published by
F. A. Thorpe (Publishing) Ltd.
Anstey, Leicestershire

Set by Words & Graphics Ltd.
Anstey, Leicestershire
Printed and bound in Great Britain by
T. J. Press (Padstow) Ltd., Padstow, Cornwall

This book is printed on acid-free paper

1

"I'LL be a sorry son of a bitch!" Bodie said in disgust as his bullet kicked up a gout of earth at least a yard away from the man called Tarrow. He levered a fresh round into the breech, rose to his feet, and moved across the dusty ridge.

Ahead of him Tarrow suddenly stopped running, turning quickly, his own gun swinging in Bodie's direction. The manhunter threw himself to the ground as the gun blasted a spear of flame. As Bodie struck the ground, rolling frantically, he felt the vicious snap of the bullet as it burned the air just over his prone body. He came to rest, throwing his rifle to his shoulder again, this time holding his aim before he touched the trigger. The bullet caught Tarrow just as he was turning away and it spun him

1

off his feet. Tarrow hit the ground hard, his body bouncing. A gush of blood spilled from his right shoulder. He jerked himself upright, firing as he began to regain his feet. And that was when Bodie's second bullet punched a ragged hole through his chest, splintering bone and going on to penetrate the heart. Tarrow went over onto his back, legs kicking as he died.

Bodie stood up, hearing the last echoed rattle of his gunshots fade. He made his way across to where Tarrow lay. The man was already dead by the time Bodie reached him. He stared down at Tarrow, thinking that the man hadn't looked the kind who might up and slaughter a whole family just for thirty-five dollars. But that was what Tarrow had done. And he'd led Bodie a hell of a chase — all the way across New Mexico and down to this arid corner of Arizona. For thirty-five dollars! Bodie shook his head. He thought of the butchered family, the four graves where they were buried. Only the human animal could kill so wantonly for so little!

He walked back and found Tarrow's horse. Leading it to the body he draped Tarrow face down across the saddle, tying him down with his own rope. Then Bodie caught up his own mount, climbed into the saddle, and began the ride back to Ridgelow, the town he'd passed the day before. He might as well collect his bounty there, let the law in town deal with Tarrow, because sure as hell was hot, Bodie wasn't going all the way back to New Mexico with Tarrow's body.

It was mid-morning of the next day when Bodie rode in along Ridgelow's dusty main street. He paid no attention to the interested crowd of spectators who followed him all the way to the jail. At least Tarrow's ripe smell kept them from getting too close.

The town marshal was lounging in an old rocking chair on the boardwalk outside his office. He watched Bodie ride up and dismount, glancing half-heartedly at the body draped across the led horse.

"Looks like you come a fair way, mister," the marshal said, running his gaze over Bodie's dust-streaked clothing. He gave a good-natured smile. "Mind, you look in better condition than your friend."

Bodie pulled a folded poster from his pocket and tossed it to the marshal. "His name's Tarrow. They posted a bounty on him back in Las Cruces. So there he is. Read the poster. Be obliged if you'd confirm my claim and wire the marshal in Las Cruces so I can collect my money."

The marshal studied the poster, nodding to himself. "Heard about this," he said. "Things some folk'll do for money," he added, fixing his eyes squarely on Bodie.

Bodie thumbed his stained hat to the back of his head, a mirthless smile playing around the corners of his taut mouth. "I know what you mean, Marshal. It's a mean world."

"Ain't it just!" the marshal said. "All right, leave it to me. I'll have somebody take him away and bury him. Come by in the morning and I'll try and have your money ready."

Bodie nodded. He turned and picked up his horse's trailing reins.

"What name do I put on the wire?"

"Bodie."

The marshal climbed to his feet and watched the tall man make his way along the street. So that was Bodie! Now that he had actually seen the man the marshal could begin to believe all the tales he'd heard. About how hard Bodie was. What a mean, out-and-out son of a bitch he'd become since throwing away his badge and building himself a reputation as a bounty hunter. He had become a legend. The marshal walked to the edge of the boardwalk and watched Bodie turn in at the doors of the livery stable at the far end of town. He glanced along the street and saw Ridgelow going about its business. He stared at the bunch of men who had gathered near the jail, and he wondered if any of them realised who Bodie was.

"Hey, Ike," he called to a skinny man dressed in soiled, threadbare clothing. "Go on down to Nate Hawley's. Tell him, I got a customer for him."

Ike nodded. "Sure, Marshal."

"And, Ike, tell him I don't want any of his fancy coffins. Cheapest he's got!"

Ike made off down the street. The marshal made sure that the horse carrying Tarrow's corpse was secured to the hitch rail, then he went into his office, closing the door. He sat down behind his desk, deep in thought, staring out of the window. He was still there when the man called Ike appeared, followed by a gaunt, grim man dressed in dusty black. A smile touched the marshal's lips as he watched Ridgelow's undertaker pause beside the waiting horse at the hitch rail, take out a tape measure and begin

6

to size up Tarrow. Nate Hawley took his work very seriously. He had a proper respect for the dead, which, the marshal admitted, was all right. The trouble was, Hawley tended to carry his professional manner into his private life. It didn't make for very cheerful conversation with the man.

The office door opened and Ike stuck his head in. "I brung him," he said.

"Thanks, Ike." The marshal beckoned Ike into the office. "Something else you can do for me."

Ike grinned with self-importance. "Sure, Marshal."

"That young woman who came to see me yesterday. The one who took a room at the hotel. Take a walk over there and ask her would she like to come and see me."

"All right."

"Ike. Just tell her I might have an answer to her problem."

Ike's head bobbed as he digested the message. I'll tell her. Marshal."

"When you get back, Ike, I'll have a

7

couple of dollars for you."

Ike left the office with all the dignity of a diplomatic courier off on a matter of national importance. The marshal followed him outside and stood watching as Nate Hawley finished writing Tarrow's measurements in a little black book. The undertaker was as fussy as a tailor measuring someone for a suit.

"Hey, Nate," the marshal said.

"Yes, Marshal?"

"I think you overlooked his inside leg!"

The look on Hawley's face was more than the marshal could bear. He turned and went back inside his office, barely managing to close the door before he doubled up with laughter.

2

BODIE had bathed, shaved, dressed in clean clothes and eaten. Later he had returned to his room at the hotel with a bottle of good whisky and some fine cigars, prepared for a session of doing nothing at all. So he was mildly annoyed when his siesta was disturbed by a knock on his door.

"Yeah, I'm coming," he growled, swinging his legs off the bed. He crossed the room in long strides, yanking open the door, prepared to air his feelings to whoever it was in the hall.

For one of the few times in his life Bodie was left speechless. For a full three or four seconds he just stood and stared. And it was the girl who spoke first.

"May I speak with you, Mr Bodie?"

Bodie took the thin cigar from his mouth. "I don't see why not," he said, and stood aside to let the girl in. He closed the door and moved across the room to pull a chair from the wall for her. The girl sat down, slim hands resting in her lap.

"The marshal suggested that I come to see you," she said. "He made no promises, of course."

I'll have to thank the marshal, Bodie thought, watching the girl. She was nothing less than beautiful. Yet there was no artificiality to her. The youthful face bore no make up, the long mass of dark hair shone with natural highlights. Bodie judged her to be in her mid-twenties, the supple body firmly matured beneath the snug fit of her brown dress. Full, well rounded breasts thrusting out above a slim waist. Strong hips flowing into long legs. He felt her eyes on him, studying him with a boldness that was unusual in a woman. The eyes were bright, clear, a warm shade of hazel, flecked with green, and they were eyes that probed and penetrated, and hinted at a deeper awareness of life than might have been apparent at first sight of the girl.

"Well, Mr Bodie, do I pass your inspection?" the girl asked candidly.

Bodie smiled. He'd asked for that. "In my line of work, ma'am, it gets to be a habit."

"Yes, I can understand. Oh, by the way, my name is Angela Crown, and I'm not married."

"What's wrong with the men round here?" Bodie asked. "They all blind?" He saw her eyes sparkle for a moment, and noticed too the slight flush colouring her smooth cheeks.

"Time and circumstance," she said quickly, passing over the subject. "Mr Bodie, I have a proposition to put to you."

Coming from such an attractive female, in his hotel room, it could have been extremely interesting, Bodie thought. But he had a feeling that from this particular young woman it was going to be business. Straight business. And it was.

"Plain and simple, Mr Bodie. I want to hire you and your gun."

"I'm not for hire, Miss Crown. The marshal wasted your time."

Angela Crown smiled. "The marshal made it quite clear that you are not normally in the habit of selling your skills, Mr. Bodie. But he did point out that I might be able to offer you the right bait."

"Go on," Bodie said, wondering just what the hell she was about to offer.

"You're a bounty hunter, Mr Bodie. Very well then, I can show you where there are probably half a dozen wanted men."

"But in return you expect me to do some gun job for you?"

Angela nodded. "Yes. For which you will be paid, Mr Bodie."

"Let me hear what you have to say first," Bodie said. He sat on the edge of the bed. "Go ahead."

"Back in the mountains, three days'

ride from here, is a mining town called High Grade. There are a number of working mines, all privately owned. I am part owner of one of them, along with my brother. We mine copper, as do all the High Grade mines. The area is very rich in copper and it is a valuable mineral. We can sell every ounce taken out of the ground. The trouble is that High Grade is being taken over by a man so desperate to get his hands on all the copper that he's willing to kill to achieve his aim. Over the past three months High Grade has become a terrible place to live. There is violence of every kind. Men beaten, crippled. Businesses burned, property destroyed. People are threatened, bribed, blackmailed, and there isn't a thing anyone can do about it because the only law in High Grade belongs to the very man responsible for the crimes."

"Who is this man?" Bodie asked.

"His name is Jonas Randall. He owns the mine adjacent to ours. It

13

turns out that he also owns a great deal of High Grade, too. Saloons. Stores. The bank. He is a man with his fingers in many pies. Somehow he always seems to get what he wants. Gradually High Grade is becoming more and more his personal domain, and he runs the place to suit his needs."

"Why is this Randall so desperate to get control of all the copper?"

"There are vast fortunes to be made out of copper. Recent geological surveys have shown that the area around High Grade has even more of the stuff than was ever imagined. Randall has a lot of influential friends, men who wield a lot of power and money, and if he can gain control of the whole of High Grade's working, he and his cronies will become extremely wealthy."

"Well, men have been killed for a lot less than a mountain of copper, Miss Crown, so I can see you've got yourself a problem." Bodie relit his cigar, gazing at the girl through a cloud of smoke. "Why are you in Ridgelow?"

"Two reasons," Angela said. "First I came to buy supplies. One of Randall's subtle little ways of trying to put my brother and I out of business has been to deny us access to food and goods in any of High Grade's stores. He's trying to starve us out. The stores he owns won't deal with us, and the others have all been warned off. Last week one of the stores tried to supply us with what we need but Randall's men stepped in. They beat the owner so bad he'll be off his feet for weeks. Now nobody dares to lift a finger to help us. Everyone is in the same position. They could be next on Randall's list. Mr Bodie, I have twenty miners up in High Grade. Good men who have worked for my father's company for years. They are loyal and they don't want to see our mine taken over any more than I do. That's why I made the trip to Ridgelow. To buy food for them."

"It could turn out to be a risky proposition," Bodie pointed out. "Were you followed?"

Angela shrugged. "If I was I didn't see them. But it is a risk I'm prepared to take, Mr Bodie!"

"You said you came to Ridgelow for two reasons."

"Yes. I decided to fight Randall on his own terms. If he can employ gunmen then so can I. I'm determined not to let him beat me. If it's a fight he wants then he'll get one."

Bodie smiled at her angry words. "You could be falling right into his hands. If you take gunmen back to High Grade it might just give Randall the excuse he wants to wipe you out."

Angela shook her head, dark hair swinging. "What else can I do? Just stand by and let him take the company my father built up from nothing. Mr Bodie, my father was one of the first to have workings in High Grade. He had faith in the place when others did not. Now that the promise is coming true this man Randall comes along and expects to step in and take all the rich pickings. I won't let it happen, Mr Bodie! Not without giving him a damn hard fight!"

"Tell me something, Miss Crown. How many guns have you hired?"

"None," she said bitterly, eyes flashing at him. "Mr Bodie, are you laughing at me? Because if you are I'll . . . !"

Bodie threw up a big hand. "Ease off there. I'm not laughing at you. Just trying to find out what you've managed."

Angela slumped back in her seat. "Not a lot," she said softly.

"Given all you've told me," Bodie said, "what makes you think I won't just ride up to High Grade looking for these wanted men myself? I haven't agreed to any kind of deal."

"No, I understand that," Angela said. "But I don't think you will."

"I wouldn't count on it, Miss Crown. Like I said, I'm not a hired gun. I'm a bounty hunter."

"And the best there is according to the marshal. You have a reputation, Mr Bodie, and I'm prepared to pay well for that reputation and the gun behind it."

"When do you leave for High Grade?"

"In the morning. When I leave here I will be going to the store to finalise the supplies I'm buying. In the morning I'll have them loaded in the wagon I've bought, and then I'm returning to High Grade." Angela looked at Bodie expectantly. "Does this mean you'll help me?"

"No," Bodie said. "But it means that by the time you leave I'll have given you my answer one way or the other."

Angela stood up. "That is fair, Mr Bodie. Thank you for giving me your time. I will look forward to your decision."

At the door Bodie asked: "Have you ever handled a loaded wagon and team?"

"I've had a little experience with them." Angela smiled. "Taking one up a mountain will be something new, though. Good day, Mr Bodie."

Bodie closed the door. He crossed to where his whisky waited and lifted the glass to his lips. Standing by the window, which overlooked the street, he was able to see Angela Crown leave the hotel a minute or so later. She crossed the street and went into a store some way down. Bodie stood for a time then stretched out on the bed.

He found that he was unable to rid his mind of Angela Crown's image. He shut his eyes and he could still see her smiling at him, those clear, penetrating eyes staring at him. Damn the woman! He'd only known her for a short time, yet she'd already left a powerful feeling behind. Her personality kept thrusting itself on him, demanding his attention, and Bodie realised that he was going to have difficulty erasing Angela Crown from his thoughts.

He even found a growing interest

in her problem. The situation at High Grade was far from new, but to the people involved it would warrant their full attention. In the wide and empty frontier territories there were many men of Jonas Randall's breed. They were takers. Opportunists who hovered like vultures, waiting for the tasty morsels. They allowed other men the dubious privilege of sweating, of labouring, creating the wealth, and then they stepped in and took it, by force and violence more often than not. There was no-one to stop them. The law was spread very thinly over the vast territories. Many isolated communities still survived by being their own law. Administering rough justice, and not always too concerned about the finer points of law. But it was a means to an end. Until there were enough official lawmen to keep the peace, a man was still liable to dispense his own justice. Men like Randall thrived in a lawless community. They were smart enough to be their own law, using it to further their nefarious activities. It meant they grew more powerful while the smaller man was simply swept aside. Or trampled on. Or hung, or shot, or . . . the final solution hardly mattered. It all boiled down in the end to one simple fact: if you were big enough, waved a large fist, and didn't give a damn for anyone, then you were bound to get ahead.

A trip to High Grade could easily turn out to be profitable. He'd be paid for hiring out his gun to the girl, and if there were wanted men in High Grade that would mean some extra bounties. Bodie stared up at the ceiling. Why not take the job? Money was money, and he was getting short. Tarrow was only going to bring in nine hundred dollars, which wouldn't go far. The money Bodie had earned from wiping out Linc Fargo and his bunch was long gone. Bodie enjoyed the luxuries money could buy and never regretted spending it. But he wasn't too keen on not having any at all. And he needed money to survive.

He lay for a while longer, considering Angela Crown's offer. Abruptly he got up. He strapped on his gun, picked up his hat and left his room. On the boardwalk outside the hotel he took a casual glance up and down the street, seeing nothing out of place. Satisfied he made his way across the street and entered the store he'd seen Angela Crown go into.

"May I help you?" the pink-cheeked man behind the counter asked.

"Is Miss Crown still here?" Bodie asked.

The man shook his head. "She left some little while ago. On her way to the livery stable to look over the wagon she's just purchased. I believe she just wants to make sure everything's all in order for her trip in the morning," the man said. "As I said to the two other gentlemen asking for her, a very thorough young lady."

Bodie's eyes fixed on the man. "When was this?" he snapped.

"Not more than ten minutes ago. Why, I . . . !"

Bodie left the store at a run. He turned along the boardwalk, long legs covering the distance to the livery in the shortest possible time.

The livery stable and its complex of corals stood at the far end of Ridgelow, some way removed from the last building on the street. As Bodie rounded the large, main coral, he became aware of the silence surrounding the place. He had that instinctive gut feeling that told him something was wrong. Approaching the main stable he saw that the big double doors were slightly ajar, and a motionless figure lay in the straw-littered dust just inside the doors. Bodie recognised the old man who ran the stable. There was a ragged, bloody gash running across the man's bald head.

"Damn!"

Bodie stepped inside the stable, eyes adjusting to the gloom. He heard a muffled sound from somewhere deep in the cavernous building. Following on the sound came a sharp protest: a woman's voice. And then a man's excited giggle. Bodie moved quickly along the rows of stalls. He knew his instinct had been right. It never failed. It had warned him there was bound to be trouble.

3

IT had been Billy-Jack's idea to ride into Ridgelow and Pike hadn't needed much persuading. He was fed up himself, just sitting about up in the hills above the town, waiting for the Crown woman to leave. And when Billy-Jack pointed out that she was on her own it all added up to a heap of fun for the pair of them.

They were both sick of their own company. It was five days since they'd left High Grade. Five days in which all they'd done was to trail the Crown woman down out of the mountains, clear to Ridgelow. Jonas Randall's instructions had been clear enough. Follow her, and if she gets up to anything likely to cause trouble for me, make sure she doesn't get back to High Grade. It was a simple enough task. The trouble was Randall hadn't been aware that Billy-Jack and Pike were men with little loyalty or dedication. He had hired them along with half a dozen others, buying their guns but not their common sense. If he'd gone into their backgrounds he would have found out that both Billy-Jack and Pike were unreliable when it came to the kind of job he had set them.

As the pair rode down out of the hills, easy in their saddles, feeling the sun warm on their bodies, they were both looking forward to their intended encounter with Angela Crown. They had seen her around High Grade, following her movements as she had passed them in the street; watching the natural flow of her shapely young body, expressing to each other what they would like to do with her, given the chance.

The closer he got to Ridgelow the greater became Billy-Jack's sexual excitement. He was already having difficulty controlling himself. The more he tried to avoid direct thoughts concerning Angela Crown the greater was his awareness. By the time they rode in along the street Billy-Jack had a full erection and the constant action of the saddle between his legs did little to help ease his feelings. It was a problem Billy-Jack had been troubled with for a good few years, right from the time he'd first become aware of girls. He only had to look at one to start having erotic thoughts, and the outcome was always the same. In the right place and at the right time it didn't matter and there were plenty of girls who found such an instant response flattering. But there were times when it caused Billy-Jack a lot of embarrassment. He didn't figure it was going to do that today. Billy-Jack wasn't bothered over Angela Crown's feelings. The only thing mattered was getting her some place where they wouldn't be disturbed and where his aching hardness would be a vital factor. Hell, he told himself, she might even like it! There was no telling with women! They were so damn contrary.

No way a man could keep track of the way they might be thinking. He glanced across at his partner, grinning at Pike's dark scowl. That was Pike's trouble. He took everything so damned serious. Even the prospect of having a woman like Angela Crown left Pike sour-faced.

Though he wasn't showing it outwardly Pike was anticipating the confrontation with Angela Crown. The thought of her lying naked at his feet, helpless, was almost too much to contemplate, and Pike thrust the image to the back of his mind. It didn't do to become too self-indulgent. Not at a time like this.

"Hey, Billy-Jack," he said, in an effort to clear his mind. "Where we goin' to find her?"

Billy-Jack glanced round. His lean young face, with its small, always angry eyes, looked flushed. "Jesus, Pike," he snapped. "It ain't that big a town. An' there's only the one hotel." He reined in outside a salon. "Let's get a drink.

We can watch the hotel from here."

Pike nodded. As he climbed down from his horse he noticed the way Billy-Jack was acting. A grin touched Pike's lips. He peered at the front of Billy-Jack's pants, his grin widening.

"Hey, Billy-Jack," he called softly, "I figure your pecker's done gone an' died, 'cause it's awful stiff!"

Billy-Jack threw him an angry look, eyes glittering, his thin mouth working silently. He tethered his horse at the hitch rail. "Pike, shut your mouth!"

Chuckling softly to himself Pike followed Billy-Jack's slim figure inside the saloon. Billy-Jack made for the bar and ordered a couple of whiskies. They took their drinks and sat at a table by the front window. From their position they were able to look down and across the street to the hotel.

They weren't forced to wait for very long. Billy-Jack spotted Angela Crown coming out of the hotel. He watched her cross the street, then he stood up. He reached the saloon door and stepped outside in time to see her vanish into a store. As Pike joined him Billy-Jack pointed out the store.

"She's in there," he said.

"Can't do much while she stays on the street," Pike mumbled and returned to his drink.

Billy-Jack followed him and they argued the matter back and forth between the two of them, keeping their voices down in case anyone in the saloon might be listening.

"Shit," Billy-Jack said suddenly. "Sittin' here arguin' like a couple of old squaws! I'll bet she's gone!"

He got to his feet and made his way out of the saloon. With Pike trailing behind him, Billy-Jack sauntered down to the store. They eased their way inside. The store, stacked high with goods, was empty except for the owner. He stood behind the counter, smiling at them.

"Can I help you?"

Billy-Jack nodded. "I guess. We're looking for a friend. A lady. Miss

Crown? We were told she was in here."

"You only just missed her," the man said. "She's gone down to the livery."

Billy-Jack smiled, nodding. "Obliged," he said, and left the store with Pike behind him. "My, my," Billy-Jack said as they stepped out of the store, "she is makin' it so nice and easy for us!"

They strolled casually down the street, cutting across towards the distant livery stable.

"Let's make sure she's alone," Pike cautioned.

Billy-Jack spat in the dust. "What the hell do you think I am? Some kind of asshole?"

As they approached the livery the old man who ran the place showed himself just inside the big doors. He raised a thin, wrinkled hand in greeting.

"Howdy there, boys," he said. His voice was thin, reedy. "Something you need?"

Billy-Jack put on his smile again. "Lookin' for Miss Crown," he said.

31

The old man jerked a thumb over his shoulder. "She's inside lookin' at her wagon."

Billy-Jack made a play of peering into the livery stable's shadowed interior. "Whereabouts?" he asked.

"Hell, boy, you want to borrow my eyeglasses?" He cackled softly. "I can see better than that!" He turned, pointing, still chuckling. "There she is . . ."

And that was when Billy-Jack took out his gun and laid the barrel across the old man's bald head. Blood welled up out of the pulpy gash as the old man slid silently to the ground.

"You didn't see that!" Billy-Jack crowed.

They walked into the livery, making hardly a sound on the hard earth floor. At the far end of the building stood a long freight wagon, and Angela Crown could be seen walking slowly round it.

Billy-Jack nudged Pike with his fist. Pike grinned, his broad face shining with sweat. He rubbed a hand across his dry lips.

"You want to toss a coin? See who goes first?" Pike asked.

Billy-Jack giggled. "It don't make no difference. She's goin' to get it one way or another!"

They moved silently through the stable, past the row of stalls, and on to the far end. Angela Crown, engrossed in her inspection of the wagon, did not become aware of their presence for some time. When she did, turning slowly, her face registered surprise and then recognition.

"So Mr Randall did send a couple of his little errand boys after me!" she said, a mocking tone to her words. What's it to be this time? Another warning? Or more threats?"

"You got too much to say," Billy-Jack said. "A mouth like that could get you hurt. Maybe even get you dead."

Angela placed her hands on her hips, facing them squarely. "Are you man enough to do it?" she asked.

Billy-Jack coloured, anger flashing in his eyes. Then he regained control of himself. He giggled softly. "Me and Pike don't like the idea of killin' you, honey! See, what we had in mind was somethin' personal . . . you know," and as he spoke he reached down and began to unbutton the front of his pants.

A cold shock held Angela's body rigid. She took a step back, then felt the rough wood of the wagon side against her shoulders. Her eyes flickered back and forth as she sought some way of escape. But the only way out was blocked by the two men. She glanced back at them. Her heart raced. Billy-Jack, his thin face gleaming with sweat, was moving slowly towards her. The front of his pants gaped open and his right hand was clutched around his erection. Billy-Jack began to grin, thin lips peeling back from his teeth.

"Go give it her, boy!" Pike urged, moving in from the side.

Angela gave a strangled cry, lunging away from the wagon. She almost made it by Billy-Jack, but his hand shot out, fingers clawing at her dress. Angela tried to pull herself free. Cloth tore with a rasping sound, exposing her arm and shoulder. She felt herself stumble. Billy-Jack gave a grunt, grabbed hold of her by the hair and yanked her towards him. As her body came round, Angela rammed her right knee up into Billy-Jack's exposed groin. He yelped, tears filling his eyes. In a moment of hurt anger he lashed out, the flat of his hand catching the side of her face, spinning her against the side of the wagon. Angela caught hold of the wagon to support herself. Peering through the hair that had fallen across her face she saw Billy-Jack advancing towards her. He was doubled over, clutching at his groin.

"You bitch!" he rasped. "Stupid bitch!"

And then he threw himself at her, ripping and tearing at her dress, shredding it away from her body, exposing her full, white breasts. A soft cry of pain escaped from her lips as he dug his fingers into the soft flesh, deliberately squeezing the tender nipple. She kicked and struggled, knowing she was losing against his superior strength, and felt herself being forced down on the ground. Billy-Jack's weight was sprawled across her. He thrust one hand up the tangled skirt of her dress, tugging and jerking at her thin undergarments. Angela fought in silent desperation. She tried to pull away as she felt his clawing hand on her naked belly, fingers probing, exploring. Then his hand slid down to the junction of her thighs, fingers plucking at the soft tangle of pubic hair. She heard him laugh, high, and excited, triumphant sound.

The laugh abruptly changed, a new sound rising in Billy-Jack's throat. Now he was choking, gasping for breath, his face, only inches from Angela's, dark, the features taut. She stared at him, bewildered, and then she rolled her head to one side, staring up as a dark shadow fell across her.

And then she knew . . .

4

BODIE'S right foot drove forward, the hard toe of his boot catching Billy-Jack in the side, lifting him clear of Angela Crown's body. Billy-Jack began to choke, struggling to draw air back into his lungs, and even as he was doing this, Bodie had turned, facing Pike who was rushing towards him. He saw Pike's raised arm, the heavy fist driving at his face. Bodie ducked under the blow, then sledged his own right deep into Pike's stomach. Pike grunted, mouth open in shock, hands clutched over his hurt body. Bodie stepped away from Billy-Jack. He caught hold of Pike's shirt and yanked him, upright. Then he hit Pike full in the mouth, driving him back against the side of the wagon. Blood spurted from Pike's pulped lips, dribbling down his chin. He stared at Bodie through glassy eyes, not registering the manhunter's approach. It was only when Bodie hit him again that he became aware of what was happening. Bodie's hard fist clouted Pike alongside the jaw, rolling him along the side of the wagon. Pike stumbled, his legs suddenly weak. He hit the ground hard, spitting blood and fragments of broken teeth.

Billy-Jack was halfway to his feet, fumbling for the gun on his hip, as Bodie swung into a grotesque formation. The smile was still there when Bodie reached him. He slapped the gun out of Billy-Jack's hand, then took hold of his wrist and swung him away from the wagon. Unable to stop himself, Billy-Jack hurtled across the ground and smashed face first against the stable wall. A blinding sear of pain engulfed his face and blood spurted wetly from his crushed nose and a long gash over his right eye. Bodie had followed Billy-Jack, and as the man sagged away from the wall, Bodie punched him across the jaw. He hit

Billy-Jack a half-dozen times in half as many seconds. The brutal force of the blows drove Billy-Jack along the side of the wall, then stretched him his full length in the dirt.

Staring disgustedly at his bruised knuckles Bodie stepped to where Pike lay. He slipped Pike's gun from his holster, picked up the one he'd knocked from Billy-Jack's hand, and then moved across to help Angela Crown.

"You hurt?" Bodie asked her.

Angela shook her head. She seemed more interested in pulling the remnants of her dress across her breasts. Which seemed a shame, Bodie reflected idly. He slipped off his jacket and draped it around Angela's shoulders. Her eyes lifted, caught his interested stare, and her mouth hardened slightly.

"Keep looking at me like that, Mr Bodie, and I'll begin to think I might have been safer with those two!"

Bodie helped her to her feet. He watched her as she slumped against the side of the wagon, her face pale.

"You sure you're not hurt?" he repeated.

She shrugged. "Only my dignity. Honestly, Mr Bodie, I'm all right."

"Shall we go?"

"Where, Mr Bodie?"

"First to see the marshal." Bodie indicated Billy-Jack and Pike. "Unless you want this pair let off!"

Angela rounded on him with feline rage. "Let off? After they almost . . . after what they've just done? Oh no, Mr Bodie, I certainly don't want them let off!"

"Back off," Bodie said. "I'm on your side."

Angela relaxed a little, but there was still an anger burning in her eyes. She brushed stray hair away from her face. "If you had any doubts concerning my story, this incident should clarify the situation."

"Why do you think I'm here?" Bodie said.

"You mean you knew about these men?" Angela asked.

41

"I was looking for you. So were they from what I learned."

"So it seems I am in your debt, Mr Bodie." Angela smiled. "Thank you for what you did. I won't forget it."

Bodie drew his gun as he crossed to where Billy-Jack and Pike lay. None too gently he prodded them into movement with the toe of his boot, eventually getting them up off the ground.

"We'll take a walk, boys," Bodie said. "Up the street to the marshall's office. See if he's got a couple of quiet cells were you can lie down."

Billy-Jack stared at Bodie defiantly, his face sticky with blood and dirt. "Who the hell says so?"

"I do," Bodie said. He let Billy-Jack see the cocked gun he was holding. "Now, I get any kind of crap from you, boy, I'm going to let this trigger go and blow that pecker of yours right off!"

Billy-Jack stared down at the open front of his pants that exposed him for all to see. He glanced up at Bodie, and getting the message that Bodie meant every word he said, Billy-Jack suddenly decided that the most important thing was to button up his pants.

Billy-Jack and Pike took the reluctant lead of the small procession that moved out of the livery and up the street. At the door they paused while Angela and Bodie helped the old man who ran the place to his feet. Though hurt, the old man was madder than a wet hen, and he threatened the pair of gunmen with everything he could think of from simple hanging to castration with blunt wire cutters, begging the lady's pardon. He fell in beside Bodie as they carried on along the street, finally reaching the jail. By the time they got there an interested crowd had gathered — for the second time that day.

The marshal glanced up from his paperwork to find his office crowded fit to bust. He looked from face to face, taking it all in, and wondering what the hell had happened to Ridgelow.

"You got rooms for these two?" Bodie

asked, indicating Billy-Jack and Pike.

"I guess," the marshal said. "We got charges?"

"Damn right we do!" the old man from the livery yelled. He stuck his head across the desk, jabbing a finger in the direction of the bloody gash. "See what the bastards done to me? Like to killed me!"

The marshal grunted. "Clem, If I was you I'd get off up and see the doc. Get him to take a look at that. Then later you can come by and make out a statement."

The old man nodded, eyes fierce as a swooping vulture. "Damn right I will!" he snapped. "Throw the goddam book at 'em!"

After the old man had gone, closing the door behind him with a bang hard enough to tear it from its hinges, the marshal sat back. "Let's get on with it," he said.

"Assault and attempted rape on Miss Crown," Bodie said.

The marshal's face hardened. "That

right, Miss Crown?"

Angela nodded. "If it hadn't been for Mr Bodie turning up when he did . . . " There was no need for her to say more.

The marshal stood up. He snatched a ring of keys from a hook on the wall and led the way through to the cell block at the rear. Unlocking the first cell he stood aside and let Bodie push Billy-Jack and Pike inside. The marshal locked the cell and followed Bodie back to the office.

"Would you like a drink, Miss Crown?" the marshal asked.

Angela shook her head. "I'm fine now, Marshal. Really."

"I'm sorry this had to happen while you were visiting Ridgelow. We don't normally have problems like this."

"I'm afraid this is something which has followed me from High Grade," Angela said.

"Well, they won't be going back," Bodie said.

"Hell, no," the marshal agreed. "I've

got enough to hold 'em for trial."

"You might have them locked up for a while," Bodie pointed out. "On account of the main witness leaving town in the morning."

The marshal grinned. "It'll be a pleasure to keep that pair locked up. For the rest of their damn lives if I could find reason enough."

"Have a look through your wanted dodgers," Bodie suggested. "You'll find your reasons there."

The marshal pondered on the thought for a moment. "Come to think of it," he said, "one of 'em did look familiar. What're they called?"

"Billy-Jack Struthers and Pike Cooly," Angela said. "They both work for Jonas Randall."

The marshal glanced at Bodie. "Appears to me, Bodie, that Miss Crown has put you in the picture concerning High Grade."

Bodie didn't answer, but Angela nodded. "I put my proposal to Mr Bodie."

"And?" the marshal asked.

"At the moment I am waiting for his decision."

"Hell, no," Bodie said quietly, "I'm waiting for your word, Miss Crown."

"Angela stared at him, puzzled. "About what?"

"Time we set out in the morning!"

Angela smiled at him, then glanced at the marshal. "Does that answer your question, Marshal?"

"Yes. But it don't do a thing to console me."

"Over what?"

"Over the fact that I ain't coming with you. That's a pity, 'cause I got a feeling that High Grade is shortly going to be one hell of an interesting place to be."

Bodie took Angela's arm and steered her towards the door. Over his shoulder he said, "Marshal, I don't know what you mean!" But it wasn't the truth. And even if he hadn't known fully he would have had a good idea.

5

THEY were two days out of Ridgelow and high up in the barren, sun-bleached hills. On all sides lay serried ranks of dun-coloured rock. The terrain was a great sprawl of sameness. Rock and dust, ravine and cliff. Smooth slopes of weathered stone, wind-scoured, crumbling ridges. Here a silent canyon, empty and shimmering with the trapped heat radiating down out of a sky so blue it hurt the eyes. And in all the time they had been travelling they hadn't seen another living soul or heard any voices other than their own.

The fact that they seemed to be alone worried Bodie more than anything. He instinctively mistrusted outward appearances. The further they travelled the greater became his unease. This man Randall, who had been astute enough to send a couple of men after Angela Brown, would keep the borders of his domain well patrolled. Bodie figured that by now he and Angela were close enough to make contact with those guards. It could mean trouble at any given moment. More than likely Randall's men would be the shoot-first-question-later type. Which didn't bother Bodie too much. He could give as good as he got. Maybe better.

Mid-morning of the third day found them on a thin trail clinging to the side of a towering cliff. The trail, dusty and loose-surfaced, was only just wide enough to take the heavy, loaded wagon and its four-horse team. If Bodie had fostered any misgivings concerning Angela Crown's capabilities as a teamster, they were swiftly dispersed. She handled the wagon better than most men, negotiating the trickiest stretches of ground with an apparent lack of concern. So when they found themselves on the narrow cliff trail, Bodie rode a little way ahead, scouting the surrounding area, knowing that he could leave the wagon to Angela.

And that was the way it went. Smoothly, without a hitch. Until some son of a bitch started shooting at them with a rifle!

It was Bodie who called the hidden rifleman a son of a bitch. He added a few other choice insults, too, but after that he found he was too busy trying to control his spooked horse to waste time on name calling.

The rifleman didn't appear to be trying to actually hit them. Either that or he was the worst shot ever to pull a trigger. Even so, there were a lot of bullets coming their way. They howled off the rockface at Bodie's back, making a hideous noise as they whined off into the sky. Bodie managed to get out of his saddle, dragging down on the reins to keep the horse from rearing back over the edge of the trail. There was a long drop on the far side of the trail and Bodie didn't fancy taking the quick way to the bottom.

He managed to drag his rifle from the saddle sheath. Jamming it between his arm and body he worked the lever, jacking a shell into the chamber. Sweat was already oozing from his pores, what with the effort of trying to calm his horse and being covered in fine, choking dust. There was also the added threat of being crushed against the side of the cliff by the solid bulk of his jittery horse.

Down on one knee Bodie scanned the surrounding terrain, smiling grimly as he pinpointed the rifleman's position. Each time the man fired he showed himself briefly. And there was also the telltale burst of powdersmoke.

Letting go of his horse's reins Bodie put his rifle to his shoulder, waiting for the rifleman's next appearance. He didn't have to wait long. There was a flash of colour against the dull rock on the far slope, the gout of smoke as the rifle exploded.

In the fraction of a second following the shot, Bodie touched the trigger of his own weapon. The rifle blasted a spear of flame, the sound of the shot slamming back and forth between the rockfaces.

A further shot added its noise to the rolling echoes. It came from the other man's rifle — but now the muzzle was aimed skywards, and the man himself was falling forwards, slipping loosely over the ledge of rock he'd been hiding behind. For a brief moment he hung suspended, then all at once, like some floppy doll, he slithered across the bare, sloping rock, gaining momentum before he spun out into empty space. He fell, striking rock far below, leaving a great red smear on the paler stone.

Bodie got to his feet, eyes scanning the close area in case there were more. His search revealed nothing — but, as before, that didn't mean a thing.

"Mr Bodie?"

Bodie made his way along the trail. He found Angela, a rifle in her slim hands, concealed behind the wagon.

"Somebody doesn't like us," Bodie commented. "Is this the way everybody gets welcomed to High Grade?"

"Jonas Randall is no fool," Angela stated. "He wouldn't stake everything on Billy-Jack and Pike. He'd want someone else, closer to home, to watch for me in case I managed to get this far."

"Sounds like a man who covers all his bets." Bodie helped her back on the wagon, then returned to his horse. As he settled in the saddle he glanced over the edge of the trail. Below he could see the crumpled, bloody body of the would-be ambusher.

"Mr Randall ain't going to be to pleased about you, feller," he murmured. "Not with you falling down on the job and all!"

They moved on, slowly picking their way along the trail. Shortly it opened out into a high, flat plain. There was grass here, even a few trees. Bodie spotted water gleaming through the intertwined branches.

"We'll stop here a while," Bodie said. "Let the horses rest. You want to fix something to eat?"

Angela pulled the wagon to rest close to the bank of the shallow stream. She set the brake and climbed down off the seat.

"Something on your mind, Mr Bodie?"

He glanced at her. Damned if she didn't figure his every move! That was the trouble with a smart woman. Always having to prove just how good she was.

"I want to take a ride back. Have a look at that feller." Bodie twisted round in his saddle. "Pretty open hereabouts. Not much chance of anyone sneaking up on you. I'll be back as soon as I can. You have any trouble you start shooting and we'll worry later."

Angela was opening one of the supply boxes fixed to the side of the wagon. "Don't worry about me, Mr Bodie. If I see something I don't like the look of you'll get to hear about it!"

Bodie nodded. He reined about and put his horse to a fast trot, cutting away from the marked trail. He soon found himself riding down through the rocky fall of land that would eventually bring him to the base of the high cliff they had just negotiated. It took a good half-hour to reach the bottom. Once there Bodie had little difficulty in locating the body of the man he'd shot.

The body lay wedged against a jutting outcrop of stone. The long drop and eventual contact with the rocks had finished what Bodie's bullet had started. The man's body had burst open like some huge, ripe fruit, and there was a lot of blood and pulped flesh spread across the surface of the rock. Oddly the face itself was hardly marked, though the back of the man's skull had split wide open. Bodie took a good look at the face, memorising the features before he returned to his horse and backtracked along the rocky cliff bottom, up the long slope, and returned to where he'd left Angela.

She had a fire going and food cooking. A pot of coffee threw its aroma out to reach Bodie as he drew rein. He eased from the saddle, looking for Angela. She wasn't in sight and he felt a momentary rise of alarm. Then he heard the sound of splashing coming from the direction fo the stream. Bodie tethered his horse and crossed to the bank, pushing his way through a tangle of brush edging the water.

"Coffee's boiling over," he said, taking off his hat and scrubbing his hand through his thick hair.

Angela Crown's head came round with a snap, eyes blazing, soft mouth set in an angry line. She was up to her thighs in the middle of the stream as naked as the day she'd been born, her supple body gleaming wetly in the bright sunlight.

"Mr Bodie, I'm beginning to believe you're a Peeping Tom!"

Bodie inclined his head, his face set. "Miss Crown, you could be right.

Trouble is I never have been able to control myself. Seems like my ma was right. She must have told me a hundred times if I didn't stop doing it I'd get into bad habits!"

Still glaring at him over her shoulder Angela reached up to push a stray lock of hair back into place. She began to speak, but her lips formed instead into a smile.

"I'm inclined to think your mother was right," she said, and Bodie was quick to notice that some of the frost had left her voice.

"You got to admit, a pretty woman's like a piece of nature. Man who sees it, well, he's just naturally going to take a look." Bodie turned and headed back to the cookfire.

"Mr Bodie . . . " Angela's voice drifted in his direction.

"Yeah?"

"Would you bring me the towel from on top of my travelling bag please?"

Bodie stepped across to the wagon. He spotted Angela's clothes folded in a neat pile and beside them her bag, with a large towel laid over the top. He picked up the towel and went back to the steam. Standing on the edge of the bank he held the towel open.

"Thank you, Mr Bodie," Angela Crown said. She turned slowly, her eyes fixed on his expressionless face, and walked out of the water. A faint flush of colour marked her smooth cheeks as Bodie's eyes travelled appreciatively over her naked body. Water spilled in crystal drops from her long thighs, glistened on the youthful swell of ripe breasts, nipples erect from contact with the chill stream. She flicked water from her flat stomach, fingers barely missing the dark triangle of hair at the junction of her thighs, and then she turned her back on him, allowing Bodie to place the towel around her slim shoulders.

"Thank you for the towel," she said, then followed him towards the fire. "And for the compliment."

Bodie brought two cups and poured coffee for them both. Angela seated herself across the fire from him, still wrapped in the towel. She took the cup he handed her and drank.

"That tastes good," she said. For a moment she studied him seriously, her smooth brow furrowed. Then: "I can't go on calling you Mr Bodie!"

"Just — Bodie," he said. "It's enough."

"How enigmatic," Angela observed. "Are you a man of mystery, Bodie?"

"He laughed. "Hell, no! Just a man doing his job."

"There are men and there are men," Angela declared. "Some are like blades of grass. Identical. Unremarkable. And then there are men who stand apart. They do it with such ease you can't avoid noticing."

"And?" Bodie asked.

Angela laughed, the sound light and natural. "And you are one of those who stands apart. I'm right aren't I, Bodie?"

Bodie drained his cup and reached for a couple of plates. He spooned out beans and slices of bacon. Handing one of the plates to Angela he said, "You're talking over my head, Angela Crown. I'm just a simple feller. More than happy just watching you bathing in that stream."

"And is that as far as you go, Bodie?" Angela asked. "I mean, just watching?"

Bodie coughed as he almost choked on a mouthful of beans. There she went again. He glanced at her. Angela was eating slowly. As though she'd had nothing to do with the bold question just asked.

"A question like that, Angela Crown, is liable to lead to a lot of complications. Maybe we be better to leave it unanswered a while."

Angela put down her plate. "My mother had a saying, too. There's no time like the present. Have you heard it?"

Bodie nodded. "Yeah. I figure it's got a lot going for it."

She leaned across the space between

them. "So there we are," she said very softly.

"You sure you know what you're saying?" Bodie asked, not in the least surprised at the warm ache rising in his groin.

"Bodie, I always know what I'm saying. I wouldn't be running a business if I couldn't make decisions and stick to them."

And there I thought you'd hired me for my gun," Bodie said dryly.

Angela made a slight movement with her shoulders, letting the towel slide down her body. "Bodie, you're a hard man!"

He couldn't hold back a grin at that. "You don't know how right you are," he said.

Angela came and knelt before him, slipping her bare arms round his neck. Her face tilted up towards his, her lips soft against his own. A warm sigh whispered from her throat as she kissed him, swelling to an expectant groan as Bodie's arms encircled her naked body, his strong hands caressing the supple curve of her back, moving down to cup her firm, round buttocks. He pressed her against him and felt her urgent response as she became aware of his own hardness. Angela began to grind her hips and thighs against Bodie's groin, teasing him with her tender flesh. He twisted her off balance, lowering her to the softness of the grass edging the stream. Angela lay beneath him, her fingers busy with the buttons on his clothing, her lush breasts rising and falling fiercely with her agitated breathing. When he was naked she dragged him to her, luxuriating in the feel of his muscular body against her own. Soft ripples of sound bubbled from her lips as she felt his hands exploring the contours of her body, rising with the swell of taut-nippled breasts, then slipping into the hollow of her flat stomach. A husky gasp followed the contact of his hand with her dark pubic thatch, her sleek thighs spreading in unashamed abandon. She waited expectantly, her body quivering when Bodie entered her, thrusting firmly into the soft warmth. Angela curved her body up to meet him, gripping him with long, powerful legs. She gave herself completely to the moment, letting his surging drive carry her with it, enjoying to the full every penetrating thrust, letting it build and swell, until it culminated in a long, warm flowing explosion that spread through her whole body, making her cry out in delight before it ebbed, slipped away, leaving her in drowsy comfort, locked in his arms, content for the moment.

6

BODIE had taken a quick turn in the clear water of the stream before dressing. Now he sat beside the fire, his cup of coffee refilled, a thin cigar between his lips, and watched while Angela pulled on her own clothing. His close scrutiny didn't seem to bother her in the least.

"Was it as good as you expected?" she asked candidly, coming to kneel beside him.

"You ask the damnedest questions," Bodie growled. "Men must run a mile when they see you coming."

She laughed, a soft, throaty sound. "As long as the ones I really want stay put, I won't complain. Are you going to answer me?"

"What gives you the idea I was expecting anything to happen?"

"I saw it in your eyes. Back in

Ridgelow. When you'd dealt with Randall's men."

Bodie couldn't deny it, even to himself. It took no effort at all to recall the way she'd looked. Sprawled out on the stable floor, her dress torn away from those ripe breasts, skirts thrust high around her hips. And he had wondered, in that moment, what she would be like.

"I don't think you want me to tell you really," he said.

"Why not? Is it so wrong for a woman to want to know if she's satisfied a man?"

Bodie sighed. "I'll let you know next time."

"At least that's answered my question," Angela said. She smiled indulgently, climbing to her feet and crossing to the wagon.

They began to prepare to move off. When they were set Angela climbed onto the wagon, taking up the reins. She watched for Bodie to settle in his saddle, caught his quick nod, and they set out. Bodie scouted around for a while then drew his horse level with the wagon.

"I've got a question for you," he said.

Angela glanced at him. "Yes?"

"As far as you know, when you left High Grade and set out for Ridgelow, did anyone have any knowledge as to why you were going?"

"No. I'm pretty sure of that. The only ones who knew my reason for visiting Ridgelow were my brother, Raymond, and myself. We told no-one else."

"All right. So Randall found you'd gone and sent Billy-Jack and Pike after you. He had no idea why you were going, so Billy-Jack and Pike were looking for the reason."

"I don't follow what you're getting at, Bodie."

"Randall had no proof that you were doing anything that might harm him. So he had to tread water until he knew. If Billy-Jack and Pike hadn't got over-enthusiastic about you, and tried to pull that stunt back in Ridgelow, even they would have been able to figure out what you were doing."

"Agreed. Go on."

"So as far as Randall is concerned he still doesn't know what you are up to. And he won't know until you drive that wagon down High Grade's main street."

Angela frowned. "Yes?"

"So why did he plant a gunman on that cliff trail? And why one who blazes away like crazy the minute he sees you?"

"I did wonder about that myself," Angela said. She eyed Bodie sternly. "I guessed something had been on your mind. What is it?"

"If Randall wanted a hired gun to do some shooting he'd pick a professional. One who wouldn't have missed the way our boy did."

"And what makes you think he wasn't a professional?"

"How many gunslingers do you know

who double-up as miners in their time off?" Bodie asked.

"Miners?"

"Remember, I went back to have a close look at him. He was wearing the kind of clothing miners prefer. Thick shirt and pants. Heavy, laced boots. His hands were rough. Scarred. Calloused. Not the hands of a professional gunman."

"But Randall wouldn't hire someone like that!" Angela said. "Not with all the gunmen he has around the place."

"This feller was around forty. Dark complexion. Broad jaw and cheekbones. Thick black hair brushed straight back. Nose looked as if it had been broken a few times. Scar about an inch long just under the left eye. I'd say he got into a lot of fights. Think you might know him?"

"I think I do," Angela said. "Janos Kopek. I think he was Hungarian, or Polish. Something like that. He'd been around High Grade for three or four years. Worked in the mines when he wasn't on suspension for brawling. He couldn't keep off the bottle. Always drunk when he wasn't working. He'd been fired so many times it was becoming something of a joke."

"Any chance of him having a grudge against you?"

She shook her head. "No. He never actually worked for us. For most of the other companies, but not ours. I suppose one day he would have asked for a job."

"Not any more," Bodie said.

"You think someone hired him to . . . kill me?"

"Seems that way. Man like that would be pretty easy to buy. Give him enough money for drink to last him six months and he'd shoot the president."

"Then if it wasn't Jonas Randall, who was it?"

"You got any other enemies?" Bodie asked.

Angela shook her head. "With Randall

throwing his weight around High Grade, everyone has reason to be friendly with the rest. And we've always got along with the other mine owners. Bodie, I can't think of anyone."

A couple of hours later they were easing down a long, rutted slope. Dust rose in their wake, staining the clear air. The rugged hills shimmered with heat. Bodie put his horse alongside the wagon again.

"Remember we figured that Randall might have others out looking for you?"

"Yes. So?"

"Kopek wasn't working for Randall. I think we can assume that now."

Angela studied him, puzzled. "Bodie, stop being vague."

"Kopek wasn't Randall's man. That means we're still due a visit."

"How can you be so sure?" Angela pointed out.

"Because if I'm not mistaken, they're riding in right now!"

Angela looked up, a shocked gasp rising in her throat as she saw three riders coming toward them. She hauled in on the reins, halting the wagon. Setting the brake she leaned forward to study the approaching riders, waiting apprehensively until they came into her range of vision.

"You're not mistaken, Bodie," she said. "They work for Randall."

"I know the one in the middle," Bodie said. "Sam Tucker. Can't put names to the others."

"The tall one on the left is Yancy Cree. He has a crippled right hand. Always wears a black glove over it. But he's supposed to be better than most using his left. The other one, wearing the long moustache, is Floyd Brown. I saw him beat two hefty miners in a fist-fight. When he'd done neither of the miners could stand. It was horrible to watch."

"All right. Leave this to me. Don't say a word. Just sit. But if any shooting starts you get the hell off that seat and under the wagon. Right?"

Angela nodded. "Yes. Bodie, don't

you go getting yourself shot. Not now I'm just getting to know you."

"Shut up," Bodie said. "Only a damn woman could think about sex at a time like this!"

"Brute!" Angela whispered, but Bodie had already eased his horse away from the side of the wagon, riding out a few yards to meet the oncoming trio.

They drew rein, the one named Yancy Cree pulling his horse a little to the fore. He was long and lean, with thick, corn-yellow hair spilling out from beneath his black hat. He had his reins clasped awkwardly in his stiff right hand, a thin, black glove drawn over the crippled fingers. He stared beyond Bodie, watery blue eyes fixing on Angela's tense figure.

"Nice to see you back, ma'am," he said, grinning, and exposing large square teeth.

"Something I can do for you?" Bodie asked. "If there ain't we'd like to be on our way."

Yancy Cree drew his eyes from

Angela, turning them on Bodie. The grin faded from his face. "I weren't talkin' to you, boy," he stated, his voice developing a heavy southern twang.

"Well, I'm talking to you, Cree, so listen. If you figure you got any dealings with Miss Crown, put them to me. The way I see it there ain't a damn thing between us, so I'd advise you to back off and let us through. And that ain't just horseshit I'm talking."

Brown, the one with the thick moustache, gave a low chuckle. "Looks like the lady done hired herself a tough one, Yancy! Wonder how fast he'll crack?"

"Maybe we'll find out," Cree said. "He don't sound too tough to me."

"I was you, Cree, I'd step light," Bodie advised. "You ain't chasin' niggers round the plantation now. Push a man around out here, he's liable to push right back."

"You bastard!" Cree hissed, his face flushing with anger. "I'm goin' to enjoy taking you apart!"

73

"How in hell did Randall find scum like you?" Bodie taunted. He knew for a fact that there was no way he was going to talk his way out of trouble. Not with men like these. So if it was heading for a fight he wasn't going to lose anything by trying to gain an edge. "Hell, he must have kicked over his spittoon, and there you all were!"

Oddly it was Sam Tucker who broke first. With an angry yell he twisted round in his saddle, snatching at the gun on his right hip.

"To hell with Randall," he shouted. "I ain't takin' that from no son of a bitch!"

His gun was only halfway clear of the holster when Bodie's hand dropped, gripped and lifted the heavy Colt, dogging back the hammer even as the gun was sliding free. As it levelled on Tucker the hammer was dropping again. The Colt blasted a single shot, the bullet ripping a bloody hole through Tucker's throat. A thick gout of blood sprayed from the ragged wound, more spewing from the bullet's exit hole just behind Tucker's left ear. Tucker screamed as he went back out of his saddle, falling towards the hard ground. Even before Tucker had started to fall, Bodie had left his own saddle, rolling over to the left side of his horse. He hit the ground on his shoulders, rolling to get clear, and came up shooting. He picked his target and triggered two quick shots. Floyd Brown was caught partway off his horse. Both bullets took him in the back, between his shoulders, throwing him, forward against his horse. Losing his grip Brown fell back, one foot caught in the stirrup. His horse, startled by the sudden crash of gunfire, bolted, dragging Brown's bloody body across the hard ground. It finally came to rest a couple of hundred yards away, Brown's body still dangling from the stirrup. The flesh of his face and body had been gouged and ripped as he bounced and scraped along the ground, blood streaming from ugly gashes.

The instant he'd fired at Brown,

Bodie had twisted about, seeking Yancy Cree. He heard the solid blast of a shot and felt something rip a bloody swathe across the back of his left shoulder. Dropping to a crouch Bodie half-turned his body, swinging the Colt round, and caught a blurred glimpse of Cree as the gunman raced away from him. Bodie saw that Cree was pushing his horse toward the wagon. He swore bitterly, bringing up the Colt and firing in one single movement. Cree's horse screamed as Bodie's bullet tore through its neck. It took a couple more steps then faltered, blood spraying from its nostrils. Its head went down and it crouched sideways, spilling Cree from the saddle. Cree managed to land on his feet and he continued to run forward in the direction of the wagon. He snapped off a single shot at Bodie who threw himself to the ground, bracing himself with his left hand as he struck. Bodie's gun came up, finger jerking on the trigger. The bullet took a bloody chunk from Cree's shoulder. Bodie fired again, his last shot, and even as he pulled the trigger he knew he'd missed.

But not completely.

The bullet cleared Yancy Cree's moving figure by a couple of feet, then struck the thick iron rim of one of the wagon's wheels. Flattened out of shape the bullet was deflected from its original trajectory with a vicious howl. And Yancy Cree ran straight into its path. The chunk of lead caught him just under the right eye, shattering the cheekbone into ragged splinters. Then it drove on up through his skull, into the soft brain mass, impacting against the rear of the skull, and tearing out a huge, gory hole. Cree's dying body ran on for a few more yards before he smashed limply to the ground, arms and legs flailing loosely.

Bodie climbed stiffly to his feet, walking slowly towards the wagon. He felt a soft churning sickness in his stomach. Reaction to the violent events and the pain from the burning wound

Cree's bullet had opened across his shoulder. Even as he moved he could feel the sticky blood flowing down his back.

He spotted movement by the wagon and moments later Angela stepped into view. She came towards him, concern showing on her face.

"My God," she whispered. "I can't believe what I saw! It happened so fast! One minute you were all talking . . . and then that man Tucker went for his gun . . . and . . . " She shuddered. "So quickly . . . "

"Doesn't take long for a man to die," Bodie said.

"But why? Why did they do it?" She stared at him, her eyes clinging to him, silently pleading for an explanation.

"Because they don't know any other way," Bodie told her. "Violence is the only language they understand. It's all they have. The gun is their mark of being different, and when they meet something that bothers them they use it."

"You make it sound so simple. So normal."

"Hell, of course it's normal. It's as normal as two people making love. Men have been killing each other ever since they learned how to make a hand into a fist. And they'll be doing it long after we're dead and forgotten."

Angela sighed. "It seems to me that Mr Jonas Randall has started something which could kill us all! How long can it go on, Bodie?"

He glanced up from reloading his Colt. "As long as it takes to settle," he said simply. "Or as long as there are people still standing."

Angela turned back towards the wagon. Her gaze fell on Yancy Cree's sprawled corpse. She took one look at the ugly mess oozing from his open skull and groaned softly.

"Bodie, I think I'm going to be sick!" she said, and she was.

He rounded up the lose horses, leading them to the rear of the wagon and securing them there. Then he dragged each body to the wagon, heaving them over the saddles and tying them down, covering them with blankets. By the time he'd done, Bodie was sweating. His shoulder felt as if it was on fire. He made his way to the front of the wagon. Angela was slumped down in the shade offered by the wagon's bulk, an opened canteen of water gripped tightly in her hands. She looked up as Bodie's shadow fell across her, smiling from a pale, bloodless face.

"You see," she said, "I'm, not as tough as I make out."

"Yeah? Well, don't worry about it." He lowered himself down beside her. "How do you feel about playing nurse for a while?"

"Are you hurt?"

Bodie turned his shoulder towards her. "It ain't much but it's all mine," he said.

"Bodie, you're bleeding all over the place!" she exclaimed.

"I know," he said. "Just try and stop it."

Angela removed his shirt. She examined the wound, then climbed up on the wagon to get something to clean it with. Using water from the canteen she washed away the blood and covered the long gash with cool ointment from her bag. Finally she bound Bodie's shoulder with bandage taken from the supplies she was carrying to High Grade.

"Is that better?" she asked, watching him put on his remaining clean shirt.

"Fine," Bodie said.

"When we get to High Grade I'll take you to see the doctor." She smiled wryly. "We have a very good doctor in High Grade. He should be good, because he gets a lot of practice!"

Bodie tucked in his shirt. "Way things keep happening," he said, "he's going to be getting some more!"

Angela stared after him as he moved to where his horse waited. The way he'd spoken, she thought, made it sound less like an observation and more like a very solid promise.

7

IT was exactly an hour before noon the following day when Bodie and Angela Crown reached High Grade. Angela took the loaded wagon along the rutted, thronged main street, Bodie following along at the rear, leading the three corpse-laden horses.

As they eased along the dusty street, with the hard glare of the sun beating down on them, Bodie took his first look over High Grade, and wasn't impressed in the least. High Grade was no better or worse than any mining town. It was dirty and cluttered, its buildings raw and jammed together on an uneven stretch of ground clinging to the side of the dug-over, blasted-apart, timbered-up mountain. From a couple of miles out Bodie had begun to notice the dark holes burrowing into the face of the high slopes: the mines, with their dust-streaked workers scurrying about like so many ants. The mines ranged from simple two-man operations up to the organised company workings. The small mines had crude notices stuck in the earth saying: Lucky Lady Mine. Keep Out! When the bigger mines started to worry over their property they erected high fences, strung with barbed wire, and their warning notices left no doubt as to their meaning: Private Property. Stay off Or Be Shot! High Grade itself was just as businesslike. It had no time for the frills of civilisation. Everything was solid and functional. The saloons, and there were over a dozen of them, were not adorned with the usual garish decorations on the frontages. They bore a simple sign stating that drinks were for sale. The same applied to all the other businesses. A long, low building, with the smell of hot food rolling out into the street had a sign that said: Eats! On a corner a barbershop advertised: Cuts 'n' Shaves. And down a sleazy alley Bodie caught sight of a crudely-painted sign indicating a dark doorway at the rear of a dingy saloon. The spelling on the board was incorrect, but the message was unmistakable — Fuks! And that sign just about summed up High Grade for Bodie. It was crude, down to earth, dollar-hungry, and moving too fast to give a sweet damn about anybody or anything.

And it was fit to bust at the seams with people. They were everywhere. Filling the boardwalks and spilling onto the streets. Jostling, shoving, shouting men and a fair sprinkling of women too. In the main they were miners. But there were plenty of other occupations to be found in High Grade. There were gamblers, with their dark suits and pale complexions, long fingered, keen-eyed men who spent their waking hours hunched over green-baize tables, unceasingly shuffling packs of cards, counting wads of banknotes, and keeping one eye on the other players and one on the door in case they needed a fast exit. There were the con-artists too, the wheeler dealers, the men who could talk a week-old corpse into buying a bottle of long-life elixir. And there were the goodtime girls, the saloon dancers, the ballad singers, and the plain old-fashioned whores, who sold the oldest commodity on the market. They came in all shapes and sizes, and colours, and they ranged from the cheap tarts who would do it for a dollar as long as you didn't mind standing up in a dark alley with the wind fanning your butt, right up to the cream of the crop, the ladies of the night who knew every trick in the book and sent a man home after a single night thinking he'd just been to paradise and back.

There were other specialists walking the streets too, Bodie noticed. He smiled to himself when he spotted them, though it didn't take much effort. They roamed the streets like gaudy peacocks, strutting and proud. They were the gunslingers, a breed of men Bodie had little time for. He figured they were all a little crazy. As far as he was concerned they were all bent on suicide. Why else did they go around just begging for someone to challenge them? Bodie didn't subscribe to the notion that they were simply after a reputation. No man needed to be recognised that much. Not so that he had to put up his life in some totally unnecessary gun duel with some equally unbalanced halfwit. If they won and killed the other man, what then? They spent the rest of the time flitting around from shadow to shadow, scared to trust any man, living on a razor edge, waiting for the moment when the next loose gun would come looking for them. And then it started all over again. The glory and the fame and the bravado, Bodie had decided, was just a load of crap! A pile of horseshit! The only wish the gunslingers had was a death wish, and ironically it was just about the only definite end they could reach.

"There's Deeks' office." Angela's

voice broke into Bodie's train of thought. "Hey, Bodie, are you listening?"

Bodie followed her pointing finger. There, on the corner of the main intersection, stood a substantial, stone-built structure, two storeys high. It had bars on every window, a heavy double wooden door, and a fenced compound at the rear. The top of the high fence had three rows of barbed wire running around it.

"What're they expecting?" Bodie asked dryly. "Another civil war?"

"I did warn you," Angela pointed out. "Bodie, be careful. Captain Deeks is a terrible man. I'm sure he's a little mad."

"Well, I ain't too happy myself at the moment," Bodie said. "You go on. I'll come and see you after I deliver our late friends."

Angela nodded. She pointed to where the main street split into two. One section of the street ran on through the remainder of High Grade and then carried on up the mountain to where the largest of the mines were located. The other section curved off up a long hill. At the top stood a number of larger houses. This was High Grade's residential area, its Nob Hill, where all the wealthy mine owners and businessmen from the town lived.

"I live in the white house," Angela said. "The one with red gables and the redbrick chimney."

"See you later," Bodie said, and wheeled his horse across the street towards the big, grim building. It didn't have any kind of sign outside. Nothing that might indicate its purpose. That was because there was no need. The whole place advertised itself. It was the worst kind of jail, law office, call it what you would. It stood there, smack in the middle of town, like a big, bloated spider, and anybody passing by would know what that building was for, and be glad to get out of its shadow.

Bodie reined in at the hitch rail and swung out of the saddle. He tied his horse and made sure the other animals were secure, then took his rifle from the sheath. He tucked it under his arm as he crossed the boardwalk and stepped inside. He found himself in a dusty lobby, with a staircase leading to the upper floor. Straight ahead of him lay a long passage that appeared to run the length of the building. To his left, double doors, wide open, revealed a large office. Bodie crossed to the door and glanced inside. It was a big room holding a number of desks and filing cabinets. On one wall was a long gunrack. Chained on the rack were more than a dozen rifles and an equal number of cut-down shotguns. A notice board was full of pinned up sheets of paper. In a corner of the room a small stove was burning and on top stood a large coffee pot. The smell of brewing coffee filtered across the room. Three men were grouped around a desk that was noticeably larger and more expensive than any of the other desks in the room.

"I'm looking for Deeks," Bodie said loudly.

The three men stepped aside to reveal a fourth man who was seated behind the large desk. Bodie could see why the desk was large. So was the man behind it. He was big, heavy, powerfully muscled but running to flabbiness. His broad head sat on a short, thick neck that appeared to be sunk into his wide, bulging shoulders. Black hair, cropped very short, emphasised the brute power of the man who sat there, studying Bodie with dark, bleak eyes.

"That's me," the man growled. His voice was harsh, clipped, emotionless. "I'm Deeks. Captain Deeks!"

Bodie crossed the office. "Story goes you're the nearest thing they got to a lawman in this place. That right, Deeks?"

The bleak eyes turned cold, empty. The voice took on a menacing tone. "Mister, I am the law in High Grade. Don't be fooled into thinking I ain't."

Bodie permitted himself a thin smile.

"You mind showing me your papers then? You've got a commission that says you're legally appointed?"

There was a strained silence in the room. One of the men standing by Deeks' desk gave a low snigger.

"Hey, Cap, I think he wants to see your badge . . . " he began.

"Shut your trap, Ruger!" Deeks snapped. He glared at Bodie. "Look, you, I don't know what kind of crap all this is, but you better go out an' come in again! But watch what you say next time!"

Bodie's anger rose in a sudden flash. He slammed the butt of his rifle down on the top of Deeks' desk. "The only crap I see is sitting in front of me! Some fat asshole playin' lawman! Who ain't even a lawman! Just some dumb son of a bitch who doesn't even know the kind of guts it takes to wear a badge!"

For a long moment Deeks stared at Bodie, and the manhunter could see the red tide of anger flooding Deeks' face. Deeks' huge chest swelled under his tight shirt, and he suddenly gave a wild bellow. Lurching up out of his chair, he swung a meaty fist at Bodie's face. Bodie had anticipated the move, and as Deeks rose out of his chair, he eased back, driving the butt of his rifle in at Deeks' jutting stomach. Deeks gave a grunt as the hard wood drove into the soft flesh. His mouth dropped open, loose lips peeling back from stained teeth.

"Hey!" the man called Ruger yelled. He stepped in towards Bodie, his arms swinging wildly.

Bodie half turned, bringing his rifle round in a brutal chop. The side of the stock caught Ruger across the face. Bone snapped with a sharp sound and Ruger slid across the office floor, his face a mask of streaming blood and crushed features.

"Get the bastard!" Deeks' voice boomed out.

As he twisted away from the falling Ruger, Bodie saw the other two men coming at him. One of them was going for his gun, and Bodie dealt with him first. The man was too close to Bodie to be able to change direction, so that he ran straight on to Bodie's rising boot. It smashed up between his legs, impacting against his groin with a sickening thud. The man rose upon his toes, a long howl of agony erupting from his throat. He arched backwards against Deeks' desk, sprawling across the cluttered top, sending papers and files flying as he writhed in pain.

The third man rammed his shoulder into Bodie's chest, throwing his arms around Bodie's body, and the two of them slithered across the floor. Bodie slammed up against the wall, the back of his skull rapping against the hard stone. He felt the man's hard fists pounding his body and knew it wouldn't be long before Deeks himself joined in. Raising his right foot Bodie slammed it down on the other's foot. The man yelled. Bodie repeated the action. He felt bone shatter under his foot. The man let out a low sob, his arms falling away from Bodie. Bodie caught hold of the man's loose hair and yanked his head down, turning so that he was behind him. Then he shoved hard, smashing the man's face against the rough stone wall. He jerked his head back then rammed it forward again. Blood began to spatter the stonework. The man slid to the floor, his face a bloody pulp.

Behind Bodie there was a soft sound. On the floor beside him a dark shadow. A large, grotesque shadow. Deeks! In the split second he spotted the shadow Bodie heard a rustle of sound, saw the shadow raise one huge arm. Bodie ducked to one side, coming in under Deeks' arm and the heavy gun in the man's hand. He sledged a heavy blow over Deeks' ribs. The big man grunted but didn't fall back. Bodie hit him again, harder, then backed away as Deeks swung the gun like a club. The hard barrel clipped Bodie across the cheek, tearing a long gash that began to bleed heavily. Bodie realised that Deeks would be a hard man to put down.

Falling back a step Bodie took a fresh grip of his rifle, and as Deeks lumbered at him again, still swinging his own gun, Bodie lashed out. The rifle butt cracked down across Deeks' close-cropped skull. The flesh split, bright blood swelling up out of the gash and trickling down Deeks' face. Without pause Bodie hit Deeks again and again, in the same place. Deeks gave a strangled grunt. He pawed at the blood streaming down over his eyes. This time Bodie slammed the rifle into Deeks' great stomach, over and over, until Deeks, gasping for breath, fell to his knees, the gun slipping from his fingers. He knelt there, groaning, blood pouring from the ugly gashes in his skull, running down over his face, soaking into his shirt.

Bodie stepped back, panting. He touched a finger to his bleeding cheek, feeling the raw gash. It was still bleeding badly. He glanced at Deeks and swore softly. Lifting his rifle he placed the muzzle under Deeks' sagging chin and forced the man's head up.

"You hear me, Deeks?" Bodie asked.

Deeks made a low wheezing sound, blowing bubbles of blood from his thick lips. Eventually he said, "I hear you!"

"Then listen, you bastard! There are three of your boys outside wearing blankets. You take 'em and you tell your boss this is how it's going to be from now on. You tell Randall to lay off Angela Crown and her mine. She doesn't want to sell and she doesn't want any more crap from you people! Deeks, you might scare some of the poor bastards around here, but you don't scare me! You tell all your hired guns to lay off! You got competition now, Deeks. I'm setting up as law enforcement for the Crown mine, and if you figure you play hard, Deeks, just try and play my way!"

Bodie turned away and made for the door. He heard Deeks gasp out a question, and turned. "What?"

"I want to know your name," Deeks wheezed. "Who the hell are you?"

"Just tell Randall that the name's Bodie. Maybe you heard it before, Deeks. Don't worry if you haven't, 'cause you're going to hear it a lot before I run you out of High Grade!" Bodie paused before adding, "Or bury you!"

8

THE heavy pounding on the door woke Beth Arling from her light sleep. She opened one eye, frowning as the pounding continued. Damnation, she grumbled, and threw back the covers, swinging her long, shapely legs to the floor. The clock on her dressing table told her it was a few minutes after noon. Too damn early to be up and around. She felt worse for the fact that she had been indulging in her favourite dream. The dream that had been with her for a long time, and which was now close to becoming reality. Beth shrugged off the last vestiges of sleep, groping for the thin robe lying at the foot of the bed. She pulled the robe over her naked body as she made her way to the door. Turning the key she opened the door and peered wearily at the figure in the passage.

"Good Lord, you look like you seen a ghost," she said.

Raymond Crown stepped by her without a word. He crossed the room and went directly to the small table where Beth always kept a substantial supply of drinks. His hands were trembling as he uncorked a bottle of expensive whisky, spilling it as he filled a glass. Beth, closing the door, turned and crossed the room to where he stood, watching him drain the first glass and then fill it again.

"Before you drink yourself under that table, Ray, maybe you'd better tell me what's got you all worked up." Beth reached out and forced his hand away from the open bottle. "Damn you, Ray, don't play games with me!"

Raymond Crown took a couple of deep breaths. He ran a pale hand across his face. He turned to face Beth, reaching out to grasp her upper arms, fingers digging into the firm flesh.

"She's back," he rasped. "Goddam it to hell, she's back. Alive and kicking, and mad because somebody tried to kill her!"

Beth smiled. "So Kopek made a mess of it? Why didn't you listen to me, Ray? I knew I should have handled it. I must have been crazy letting you hire that drunken roughneck!" For a moment she stared at him wildly, her thoughts racing. "Does she know it was Kopek who tried to kill her?"

Raymond nodded. "But don't worry about that. Kopek's dead. And he didn't talk."

"Are you telling me Angela killed him?"

He laughed. "No. But I don't doubt she could do if the need arose."

"Then who killed Kopek?"

"You haven't heard the best part yet." Raymond said. "While Angela was in Ridgelow she hired herself a gun. He took care of a couple of Randall's men who attacked her in town and left them in jail. He shot Kopek. And he also killed three more of Randall's gunslingers who tried to interfere with Angela on the way in."

"One thing about that sister of yours, Ray. She always does things right. It's a pity that trait doesn't run in the family." Beth fell silent for a time. "Who is this one-man army."

"I haven't seen him yet. Apparently he stopped off at Deeks' office to deliver Randall's dead gunslingers."

Beth laughed. "Lord, I'd have given a fortune to have seen Deeks' fat face when that happened! Ray, the more you tell me about this gun Angela's hired, the more I think I know who it is. Did she tell you his name?"

"Yes. He's called Bodie."

Beth's blue eys gleamed with excitement. "It couldn't be anyone else."

"Do you know this man, Beth?"

"I know of him," she said. "And with a man like Bodie that's as close as you ever want to get."

"So who is he?" Raymond sneered.

"Bodie? He's the best — or worst — bounty hunter ever to have picked up a wanted poster. They call him the

Stalker on account of the fact that once he takes up chasing a man he never lets go. Not until he's buried somebody. He used to be a lawman himself a few years back. Then something happened that changed him. Right after that he started bounty hunting, and the undertakers have never had it so good."

"Great," Raymond said. "As if we haven't got enough trouble! With Bodie at her side we'll never get to Angela now!"

"Just calm down, baby, and let Beth handle things from now on."

"Yeah? How?"

"The way I've been handling things on my own for years," Beth said. "Like I said before, Ray, I should have dealt with this from the start."

"All right! All right! Don't you start lecturing me too! It's bad enough getting it from Angela all the damn time."

Beth smiled at him, slipping her arms round his lean body, pressing her supple hips against his, rubbing her thighs against his groin. "I'll bet this is one thing you don't get from that sister of yours!" She reached up and pulled her thin robe open, exposing her full, lush breasts, dark nipples rising in anticipation. "Let me take care of you, baby," she soothed. A soft groan rose in her throat as his hands reached for her breasts. Beth pressed her face against his shoulder, enjoying the caress of his eager fingers. She arched her back and let the robe slip to the floor. Smiling to herself as she caught sight of her reflection in the dressing table mirror, she eased one hand down between their bodies, quick fingers opening the front of his pants. Slipping her hand inside she grasped his swollen member, running her fingers up and down the rigid length of heated flesh. Raymond moaned softly, his body jerking. He had no resistance in him when Beth guided him to the bed. She pushed him down onto the rumpled sheets and began to undress him. And then she bent over him and made love to him, her soft lips and sharp teeth teasing and tantalising his body until he was begging her to stop. Then and only then did Beth roll onto her back, long legs spread wide for him, drawing him over her, allowing him to enter her pulsing body where he plunged frantically and uncontrollably to a swift and powerful climax, his release leaving him drained and shuddering between her legs. As always he fell asleep. Beth drew the bedclothes over them both, cradling him to her breasts, and then she began to make new plans.

First she had to have Bodie taken care of. No mistakes there. The manhunter was no raw beginner. It would take a damn good man to deal with him. Beth had such a man. If she hadn't allowed Raymond to arrange for Angela's death in his clumsy way, she would have used her man for that task as well. Mantee, her personal bodyguard, a strange and frightening creature, possessed skills far above anything the pathetic gunfighters crawling all over High Grade could never visualise. Beth had rescued him from death one terrible night, eight years back, in a stinking back alley in New Orleans. She had nursed him back to health, seeing in the giant mulatto a great potential. And she had not been wrong. From that moment on Mantee had become her devoted protector. Physically he fitted the job to perfection. Six and a half feet tall, superbly muscled, Mantee had lightning reflexes, tireless strength, and a total lack of feelings when it came to having to use violence on a fellow man — or woman. He also had a terribly disfigured face, the result of an accident during his childhood. It had left him with the left side of his face scarred and twisted out of shape. Shrivelled scar tissue extended from his naked skull down to his neck, the taut muscles pulling his features into a permanent snarl, exposing crooked teeth. The accident had also destroyed his vocal chords, leaving Mantee dumb. Not that it made any difference to his relationship with Beth. Mantee understood everything she told him and Beth in turn knew Mantee's every thought. Oh yes, she thought, Mantee would do very nicely. He would kill Bodie, and he would do it quickly and quietly, and that would be an end of it.

And when Bodie was out of the picture Beth would employ Mantee's skill to complete the plan. She wanted Angela Crown out of the way too. Because Angela stood between Beth and a lot of money. A great deal of money. More than she had ever had the chance of owning in her short but exciting life. With Angela dead, her brother Raymond became the sole owner of the Crown mines, and Raymond wanted to sell the mine to Jonas Randall. Beth wanted him to sell it, because she wanted him to have the money. Then they could leave High Grade. Once they were away from the place Beth would relieve Raymond of the money, which wouldn't be difficult.

Raymond was a weak fool. He was putty in Beth's hands, completely infatuated by her. In his own way he was as devoted as Mantee. The only difference was that Raymond could talk and seemed to want to spend most of his time between her legs. Which didn't worry Beth. She had learned early in life that being a woman meant she had a powerful hold over men. At first she'd been amazed at the lengths men would go to just spend a few hours in her bed. Then her devious mind had worked out that if she played her cards right she could turn that power into profit. Beth had luck on her side. She was young and attractive and she had a beautiful body. At fifteen, when she found herself alone in the world, her parents dead after a tragic fire, the cold reality of life slapped her in the face. But fate, in the shape of a hairy, smelly, middle-aged buffalo hunter turned up. He took Beth away from the burned-out ranch, wrapped her in stinking buffalo robes, and rode off with her across the snow-lashed Texas plain. At first she'd been grateful for being rescued. Two nights later the gaunt hunter had taken her to his blanket, and with a lot of grunting and sweating, despite the bitter cold, he had taken her virginity and her innocence. The first time Beth had been terrified. After that, with each passing night, she found it wasn't so bad after all, and by the time they reached the first town Beth realised she wasn't in such a bad way. Each time he'd had his way with her the hunter had placed a ten-dollar gold piece in her hand. On reaching the town Beth had one hundred dollars in her pocket. It was just the beginning. She learned quickly and she had a businesslike mind. By the time she was twenty Beth's bank account ran to thousands. Gone were the days of ten-dollar buffalo hunters. Beth Arling had risen in the world. Now she only chose the wealthy clients. And they were only too eager to spend their money on the blue-eyed, golden-haired beauty who wore fashionable clothes, was always clean and doused in expensive perfume. In Baton Rouge Beth befriended a forty-year-old French whore by paying off a debt the woman owed to a wealthy patron. In return the French woman taught Beth everything she knew, and Beth became aware of techniques she had never dreamed of. In the next few months Beth used her new methods, finding she was able to please and satisfy her customers ever more than before. In New Orleans she met Mantee. With him at her side she moved back out west, where gold strikes and silver strikes were attracting men by the thousand. Barely able to count or read, many of them not even able to speak the language, they were digging their way to vast fortunes. And for many of them it was enough to spend it on drink and gambling and women. So Beth Arling began to follow the strikes. With her sharp mind and her money Beth plied her trade in her own unique way. No grubby back room for her. Nor a flea-ridden blanket in the back of a creaky wagon. When Beth arrived in a new town she would look around for a saloon to buy into. Once established she would run the place with a firm hand. No crooked gambling. No cheap drinks. She offered good value in everything, attracting a lot of custom. The rest was easy. She used the saloon to pick her clients. Any man who wanted a woman didn't need to look any further than Beth. She charged highly but the client got his money's worth. And one satisfied client was the best advertisement a girl needed. The men flocked to Beth's door, offering higher and higher prices. The moment any of the towns showed signs of dying Beth would sell up and move on.

As the years slid by Beth added to her substantial bank balance. She never tired of her work. One reason was that she actually enjoyed sex. She was a woman who need ample personal satisfaction. But even so, she was wise enough to know that it couldn't go on forever. One day she would start to get old. And no amount of sexual expertise would make up for sagging breasts and flabby thighs. Beth saw that she was going to have to think about the later years. And the moment that line of thought crossed her mind she decided she didn't want to wait until she was old before she quit. She made up her mind to get her hands on some really big money. Big enough so she could move out to California. Buy herself a big house and maybe set herself up in some kind of business. She had the sense to realise that to do that she would have to make a really big killing.

And it was shortly after that when she arrived in High Grade. She bought a saloon from a bankrupt Irishman and set up her usual operation. She had only been there a month when Raymond Crown walked in one evening. He took one look at her and couldn't stay away. Within a couple of days Beth knew everything there was to know about him. Plus the most important thing.

Which was his half ownership of one of the richest copper mines in the area. She also found out about the offer Jonas Randall had made for the mine, and the pressure he was putting on Raymond and his sister Angela. Randall had made an offer close on a million and a half dollars for full control of the Crown mines. Raymond wanted to sell. He hated the mining business and he hated High Grade. But his sister didn't. She refused to even consider selling.

For Beth it was her dream come true. Here was her big killing. The kind of money she had dreamed about. So close she could almost smell it. All that stood in her way was Angela Crown. So she went to work on Raymond. Allowing him every moment he wanted with her. Which was considerable. Beth figured it worth every second. Though weak and given to self-pity, Raymond was an attractive man. At his best he might not have been the most dominant man Beth had taken to bed, but she was experienced enough to make him believe he could master her. She put on some superb performances for his benefit, writhing and moaning beneath his straining body, using every trick she'd been taught all those years ago, and through it all she was adding up the cost, smiling when she realised how little she was having to lay out for such a big reward at the end.

Over the weeks she worked carefully on Raymond's antagonistic attitude towards his sister. Cleverly she had instilled in his mind the fact that Angela stood between him and the money that would allow him to leave High Grade. She had persuaded him, convinced him, that Angela was ruining his life. And that she was stopping him from taking her, Beth, away with him. She had told him that she would never leave him. That she had to be with him. Because she needed him like she had needed no other man.

And one night, late, as they lay in her bed, bodies entwined in the heated throes of desire, Beth had offered the final solution. As she had whispered the words in his ear Raymond had jerked his head round to stare at her, his eyes wide with surprise. He had paused in mid-thrust, his whole body quivering, and a strange expression had flowed into his eyes. Beth had gripped him with her naked thighs, lifting her hips in urgent response. He had given a low, throaty moan, suddenly thrusting into her with desperate agitation. His climax had been so violent that the sheer intensity of it had driven Beth herself to her own release. Raymond had collapsed on top of her, his body shivering, gleaming with sweat, and it had been a long time before he had moved. Eventually raising his head he had stared at her again, still with that odd look in his eyes, and a wild grin had curved his thin lips. In that strange moment Beth had known, without a shadow of a doubt, that she had him. That he would agree to her suggestion to kill his sister.

The only flaw in the plan had been

Raymond's clumsy attempt to forge ahead with the plan without asking her advice. He had learned of Angela's planned trip to Ridgelow to buy supplies, and had hired the man called Kopek to wait for Angela's return and kill her out on the trail. Beth had been angry when he had told her, but she concealed her anger, hoping that Kopek managed to carry out the murder as arranged. But as she now knew, the plan had not gone as it should. Kopek had died. Angela had returned to High Grade, along with the man called Bodie, creating a further problem . . .

Sliding from Raymond's embrace, Beth eased herself out of bed. She crossed the room and pulled back the curtain. She gazed down on High Grade's busy street. The sooner she could leave this place the better! High Grade was beginning to bore her. The prospect of a peaceful life somewhere in California held greater appeal with every passing minute.

Beth padded across the room and

rapped on the wall with her knuckles. In the next room was Mantee. Her knock brought him to the connecting door. Beth unlocked it and moved to her dressing table. Seating herself on the padded stool she picked up a brush and began to tidy her hair. She heard the door open and sensed Mantee step into the room. She carried on brushing her hair.

"Mantee, there's something I want you to do for me," she said. Glancing in the mirror she saw Mantee's huge head move in a nod. "Come here," she went on, her tone soft, gentle, as if she were talking to a child.

Mantee came and stood beside her. His great bulk seemed to fill the room. She knew he was staring at her naked body, and the thought excited her. She felt her nipples pucker, start to rise, felt the warm pulse between her thighs.

"There is a man in town, Mantee," she said. "He is bad for me. He wants to spoil my plans. He must be removed."

Mantee uttered a hoarse grunt. He held out one of his huge hands, clasping it into a massive fist.

"Yes, Mantee, he must die! You must do it at night, so that no one will know it was you. Do you understand, Mantee? No one must know we are involved."

Mantee nodded. He watched as Beth stood, turning to face him. She smiled at him, reaching out to stroke his scarred face. He gazed at her in silent admiration. Beth laid her hand over his, lifing it to her breast, pressing it against the soft, warm flesh. Her nipple thrust stiffly against Mantee's palm. He cupped his huge hand over her breast, cradling it gently, as if afraid of hurting her.

"We will never leave each other, Mantee," Beth said. She took his hand and slid it down to the inviting softness between her strong thighs. "I will always protect you. And you will do what I ask. Always, Mantee! Always!"

9

"DO you have this effect on everyone you meet?" Angela Crown asked as she carefully sponged the congealed blood away from the gash on Bodie's cheek.

"No. With some people I bring out their best." His remark was directed at Angela in such a way that she couldn't stop herself from blushing.

"Seriously, Bodie," she went on. "Deeks is a bad man to have as an enemy."

"So is a little old lady if she's carrying a sawn-off shotgun. I gave him fair warning. Stay away from me and Crown property. Even a simple-minded son of a bitch like Deeks should be able to understand that."

"But Deeks takes his orders from Jonas Randall," Angela persisted.

Bodie sat back as she completed her

task. He watched her move across the kitchen, liking the way her body curved beneath the clinging dress. He picked up his cup of coffee and took a swallow. "What were you saying about your brother?"

"Ray?" Angela shook her head. "I can't understand what's come over him. When I came into the house he looked at me as if he hadn't been expecting me to come home. He really was shocked, Bodie. Then he recovered and started to argue with me. About the same old thing. That we should sell up and get out of High Grade. Take Randall's money and run."

"It'd be a way out," Bodie suggested.

She turned on him, her eyes flashing angrily. "The easy way! Oh, I know all about that, Bodie. I have to live with it every day. Ray never lets up. I'm sure now that he doesn't care what happens to the mine. But I do, Bodie. I care that my father spent years making it what it is. That there are good, honest, hard-working men keeping that mine productive. Men who stuck by my father through the bad times. They trusted him and he never let them down. I don't intend to change things now."

"Randall would keep the mine going wouldn't he?"

Angela laughed. "Oh, he'd keep it going. But he'd bring in his own people. Cheap labour. Exploited immigrants, hounded by his damn bully boys. Captain Deeks and his crew. It's the way Randall works."

"Lady," Bodie remarked, "you sure do love a fight."

She came across the kitchen to stand before him. "I just know what I want, Bodie, and I don't like having to give up." She studied him quizzically. "That's my reason, Bodie. What's yours?"

"My what?"

"You know what I'm talking about. When we left Ridgelow you'd hired on to see me through to High Grade. We hadn't really talked over what would happen after we arrived. Now, though, I'm beginning to get the feeling you've let yourself become involved. I'm glad. But I'd like to know why?"

"Likely to be a few bounties to pick up. You told me so yourself."

"No, that isn't the reason. Bodie, I've got to know you pretty well, and there's more to it than all that talk about bounty."

Bodie helped himself to more coffee. "Go ahead and tell me. I'm listening."

"Damn right you are," Angela fumed. "I said once you were enigmatic. I'm still right, but I've realised that you are also an extremely exasperating man. Still you don't fool me, Bodie. You see I know the stories going round about you. How you were a lawman yourself before you took up bounty hunting. From what I can see you're still a lawman, and the situation here in High Grade, just sticks in your throat. You just don't like it and you can't leave it alone."

Bodie fished a thin cigar out of his

shirt pocket and stuck it in his mouth. He picked up a match off the table and lit up. All the time he was doing it, his eyes were fixed coldly on Angela. Even his face had changed, the tanned flesh drawing tight over the strong bones. Angela tried to read what was going on inside his head, but there was no way she could penetrate the rigid mask. After a moment she turned away, then gasped as Bodie's big hand reached out to grasp her slim wrist. He pulled her over his lap, arms sliding round her. Then he took the cigar from his lips.

"You know what your trouble is, lady? You just don't know when to quit talking!"

"I know," she said. "What are you going to do about it, Bodie?"

"I'll figure something out," he growled. Then he changed the subject abruptly. "Where's this brother of yours now?"

Angela shrugged. "After we'd argued he slammed out of the house, said he'd be back when he showed up."

"You know where he went?"

"I can hazard a good guess," Angela said. "He has a . . . woman down in town. Beth Arling is her name. She owns a saloon, but that isn't her true profession. She's a whore. A pretty one, I'll give her that. But I wouldn't trust her as far as I could throw her. Ray is infatuated by her. I'm not supposed to know about it, but women gossip and the story got to me finally."

Bodie digested the information silently filing it away for future reference. Bit by bit, he was beginning to form a picture illustrating the different sides here in High Grade, and the more he added the less he liked the result. From the way things seemed to be moving, there was a hell of a lot more going on in High Grade than even Angela realised.

"Well, let's worry about brother Raymond when we see him," Bodie said. "I think it's time you showed me this damn mine of yours."

Angela wriggled on his lap. "And I thought you'd put me on your knee for something else!"

"Yeah? We'll worry about that later, too!"

They left the house, crossing the yard at the rear to the small stable. Here Bodie saddled a horse for Angela. She had changed into riding breeches, a white blouse and a short jacket. Once they were in the saddle she led the way from the house, cutting off across country. The mine lay about half a mile out of High Grade. The area before the actual mine entrance was fenced off and inside this compound were the living quarters for the miners, store and supply sheds, a blacksmith's forge. As Bodie and Angela rode in through the open gates a couple of loaded ore wagons rumbled slowly by them, thick dust rising from under the huge, heavy wheels.

"Things will be better when the railroad put tracks into High Grade," Angela said. "Until then the wagons have to haul the ore twenty-five miles to the railhead at Lansing's Halt."

They drew rein outside the long, low building that served as cookhouse and mess hall for the miners. As they climbed down out of the saddles a stocky, grey-haired man with a deeply tanned face approached. He wore faded, dusty clothing, heavy boots and carried a thick walking stick.

"I'm glad to see you back safe and well, Miss Angela," he said. His accent was strange to Bodie at first, the words rolling soft and rich from his tongue. "The lads will eat well tonight, thanks to you."

"You can thank Mr Bodie here, too," Angela said. "If it hadn't been for him I don't think I would have made it."

"Then you have my gratitude, Mr Bodie," the man said. He thrust out a strong hand, shaking Bodie's vigorously.

"This is Len Treval," Angela said. "He runs the mine. He was with my father right from the beginning. I don't know what I'd do without him."

"Take no notice, Mr Bodie. I do my job that's all."

Angela smiled. "You do more than that, Len, and you know it."

"You always been a miner, Mr Treval?" Bodie asked, while his gaze wandered back and forth across the compound, picking up details here and there.

"Aye, lad, and my father and grandfather before me." Treval smiled wistfully. "Though they did their mining back in the old country. In the Cornish tin mines."

"What brought you to America?"

Treval laughed. "I didn't like the troubles, lad. Bad conditions. Worse than bad employers. So I took myself to this wild country, looking for whatever it is men expect to find in a new land."

"Did you find it?"

"I was lucky. I found work with Mr Crown, and no man could have asked for a better employer or friend." Treval gazed around him, bitterness edging his tone. "But now . . . !"

"Has Randall been giving you trouble?" Bodie asked brusquely.

Treval glanced at Angela, who nodded to him. "If there's anything to tell, Len, I want Mr Bodie to hear."

"Aye, we've had one or two incidents. One of the lads got himself knocked about by a couple of Randall's men the other night. The word was put to him that it could happen again if he didn't throw up his job and leave town. And there have been some minor accidents. Deliberately caused, we've found out. This morning we found a couple of sticks of explosives at the entrance to the mine. There was a note wrapped around the fuse. It said: This fuse could have been lit."

"Oh, Len, I didn't realise. Ray didn't say a thing about them."

Treval's face stiffened and he averted his gaze from Angela. "At the time I told him, he didn't appear to be too concerned, Miss Angela. I'm sorry to have to say it, but it's the truth."

"I'm sorry, Len."

He touched her arm. "It isn't your fault, girl."

"Have you done anything about keeping the compound secure?" Bodie asked.

"The gates are locked at night, man!" What the hell else can we do?" Treval snapped.

"I'm talking about a couple of armed guards," Bodie said. He gestured across the compound. " A blind man with a broken leg could get in over that damn fence."

"Aye, man, I dare say," Treval replied. "But we're miners, not gunmen. And do you expect my lads to spend the night walking round with rifles under their arms after a full day digging in the dirt?"

Angela stepped between the two men, her eyes blazing with anger. "Now just stop it, the pair of you! We're all supposed to be on the same side."

Bodie tipped his hat to the back of

his head. "Mr. Treval, you're right."

"Hell, man, so are you. This place needs watching at night. Can you do something for us?"

"You want me to?" Bodie asked Angela.

"Yes," she said without hesitation. "I don't want any of the men hurt, so if a couple of armed guards will prevent that then find some."

Bodie wandered off across the compound, leaving Angela to talk to Treval. He made a few mental notes concerning the need to keep watch on certain sections of the compound, and he was still sizing the place up when Angela joined him.

"I think Len kind of took to you," she told him.

Bodie glanced at her, a wry smile edging his mouth. "That just about makes my day worthwhile," he said.

She scowled at him. "What an awful man you are," she said.

"They do say so."

Leading their horses across the compound they walked out through the gates. Angela was about to mount up when she turned abruptly, touching Bodie's arm, indicating a black buckboard coming down the trail in their direction. A pair of riders followed closely behind the buckboard, which had only one occupant.

"Jonas Randall!" Angela said, her voice trembling with anger.

Bodie watched the approaching buckboard. The man handling the reins took notice as he spotted Angela, and turned the buckboard towards her and Bodie. He eased it to a halt a few yards away, sliding across the leather seat so that he could lean out a little.

"Did you have a good trip, Angela?" he asked. His tone was pleasant, almost cordial. In fact his whole appearance seemed to belie everything Bodie had heard about him. Jonas Randall was a tall man, broad-shouldered, his body firm-muscled beneath the expensive dark suit. He wore a spotless white shirt and a dark string tie. His gleaming boots were handmade, the rich leather beautifully embossed. Beneath the brim of his hat his handsome face creased into a smile of welcome. "If only I'd known you were going to Ridgelow, Angela, my dear, I would have seen to it that you travelled in style."

"How?" Angela asked coldly. "In a hearse?"

"Do you know, that's what I've missed over the last few days. Your sparkling, though sometimes acid, wit. High Grade has been a sadder place since your departure."

"Well, I'm back now, Randall, so be prepared for some surprises," Angela said.

Randall fell silent for a moment or two. He stroked the side of his jaw thoughtfully. "I really do think Angela, that the time has come for you to put a stop to this hopeless resistance. Be honest with yourself. You cannot go on indefinitely. Sooner or later you are going to have to give in and meet me on my terms."

Angela shook her head slowly. "That's where you make your mistake, Randall. You've played God so many times you think everyone believes it the way you do. Well, I'm afraid it doesn't work on me. All I see is a cheap crook who doesn't care how low he has to go to get what he wants. Do what you will, Randall. But this mine is not for sale. Not now! Not ever!"

Jonas Randall sighed wearily. "I'm sorry to hear you say that, my dear. Because I shall hate having to hurt you if you happen to get in my way!"

Bodie, who had been quietly standing in the background, eased forward so that he was standing beside Angela. He waited until Randall's attention was attracted.

"Randall, you've just said the one thing I hoped you would say. Mister, I think I'm going to enjoy putting you down." Bodie glanced in the direction of the two riders at the rear of the buckboard. "And tell those two tramps to back off! If either of them even thinks about his gun I'm going to blow his head off!"

Randall studied the tall, hard-eyed man, and knew instinctively that he was dealing with the best. This was no run of the mill gunslinger.

"So you're Bodie. Under better circumstances I could have used a man like you."

"No way, Randall. You couldn't afford me," Bodie said. "I've already seen the kind of trash you hire. They say a man gets what he deserves. From what I've seen, mister, you got a bonus."

"I don't know what you're talking about, Bodie," Randall said, too quickly.

"Stupid of me," Bodie replied. "You don't know a damn thing about Billy-Jack Struthers and Pike Cooly attacking Miss Crown while she was in Ridgelow?"

"Who?" Randall asked.

"What about Yancy Cree? Or Floyd

Brown? Sam Tucker? None of them work for you?"

"Bodie, I employ a lot of men. I can't be expected to know every single one of them. Come to that, I don't hire very many myself. I leave that to other people."

"Like Deeks, you mean?" Bodie grinned. "Inclined to run off at the mouth, that feller. Hardheaded, too."

"Are you trying to imply something, Bodie?" Randall asked hotly.

"Hell, no," Bodie said. "I'm not implying a damn thing. Mister, I'm just telling you! So you listen for a change, Randall! The lady said it. The mine ain't for sale! So like the signs say, mister, stay away, this is private property!"

Jonas Randall's face darkened, his mouth forming in to a thin, bloodless line. He moved back across the seat of the buckboard and took up the reins. With infinite caution he set the team into motion and took the buckboard back on to the trail leading down to

High Grade. His two riders fell in at the rear, casting cold glances at Bodie as they rode by.

"My, Bodie, I thought he was going to have a heart attack," Angela said. She gave a little laugh. "Don't you realise that people just do not speak to Jonas Randall in that way?"

"What I don't know, I don't worry about," Bodie explained. "And even when I do, I still don't worry about it. Now let's get back to town. I've got me some hiring to do."

On the edge of town they parted company. Angela returned to the house, telling Bodie that she would have a meal ready in an hour or so. He took his horse on into High Grade, seeking out the best saloon in town. He spent some time moving from place to place until he found the one he wanted. Buying himself a drink he took it to an empty table and sat down, his back to the wall, and watched the busy throng of customers.

Bodie had been sat there for almost

half an hour before he spotted the man he was looking for. He watched the tall, lean, dark-haired man enter the saloon and cross hesitantly to the bar. The man was dressed in range clothes, with a gun hanging on his left hip. He paused at the bar to check his money before ordering a beer. With the foaming glass in his hand he turned from the bar, his eyes searching the crowded saloon for an empty seat. When the man's eyes reached Bodie's table he hesitated. That was when Bodie lifted a hand, gesturing toward one of the vacant chairs. The man held back for a minute, naturally cautious. Then he threaded his way through the busy tables. Bodie pushed out the seat and the man eased into it, placing his glass of beer on the table. He thumbed back his stained, battered hat, revealing a brown, lean face. His dark eyes were hooded, lending him a sleepy look, which didn't fool Bodie at all.

"Obliged for the seat," he said. His

voice revealed a slow Texan drawl.

"You're a long way from home," he said.

The man grinned suddenly. "One thing about bein' from Texas," he said. "You take her with you wherever you go."

"You brought a herd up?"

"Yeah. Hell, these damn miners like their beef."

"Heading back home?"

The man shrugged. "Home's where I happen to be at the time."

"So you're just loose at the moment?"

"Look, friend, I don't mind a little talk, but you're gettin' downright pushy."

"I got a reason," Bodie said, realising it was time he made his play.

"Then tell it."

"I'm looking for a couple of good men. There's a job going. Good money."

The man across the table paused, his glass of beer in mid-air. "Depends on the kind of job," he said. "I ain't so hard up I need to go an' rob a bank!"

"This is on the level. For one of the big mines."

"Which one?"

"The Crown mine."

"Ain't that the one been having a little trouble?"

Bodie nodded. "That's my job. To help sort the trouble out. But there's a chance of something happening at night. I need a couple of good men who can patrol the mine compound and deal with anything that crops up!"

"Sounds like it could be fun."

"You interested?"

The man emptied his glass. "I guess so." He held out a brown hand. "I'm Hal Benteen."

"Bodie."

Benteen eyed the manhunter for a long moment. "Heard of a Bodie. Some kind of bounty hunter. You the same feller?"

"Maybe there are two of us going round with the same name!"

"Hell, I hope not," Benteen grinned. "Damn, though, it's a hell of a way to earn a living!"

"You think so? Comin' from a feller who spends most of his time eating dust and looking up a cow's ass, that's funny!"

"I guess you could be right at that," Benteen said. "You say you want a couple of fellers?"

"Two at least," Bodie said. "You know somebody?"

"Yeah. Feller who was on the drive. Got to know him pretty well. Handles himself just fine. And that gun he wears ain't no decoration."

"Can you find him?"

Benteen nodded. "Sure. He's around town somewhere. I'll dig him out. He'll be bedded down with some female somewhere."

"All right, Benteen. Meet me up at the Crown house in an hour. It's the white house with red gables. Up the hill."

Benteen got up and left. Finishing

his drink Bodie got up and made his way out of the saloon. As he reached the door he noticed that he was being watched from the balcony running round the upper floor. A blonde-haired young woman was studying him closely. Just behind the woman were two male figures. Bodie couldn't see them too clearly because they were standing back from the balcony rail, in the shadows of the passageway. Bodie wondered briefly who the woman was, and about the identity of the two men. Then he was outside, freeing his horse and mounting up for the ride to the Crown house.

Angela had a meal ready for him. They sat at the table in the neat kitchen, eating quietly, and neither of them spoke until Angela had poured out cups of coffee.

"Did you find any help?" she asked.

Bodie nodded. "Got a couple of men coming here in a while. I think they'll do."

"Whatever you say, Bodie."

He glanced at her, noting the flat, expressionless tone in her voice. "You got something on your mind?"

"Yes. I'm worried about Raymond." Angela put down her cup. "Bodie. I just can't help it, but I'm sure there's something wrong. Something Raymond is involved in. I'm sure of it. The trouble is the more I think about it, the less I actually want to know. Bodie, I'm scared."

"I think you need some rest." Bodie said. "After the trip and everything that happened, you need plenty of sleep."

Angela got up. She came round to where he sat, slipping her arms round his shoulders. "Will you stay with me, Bodie? I think I'm going to need you!"

Bodie heard horses in the yard. He got up and crossed to the window. Hal Benteen was just tethering his horse. He had another man with him. Bodie opened the kitchen door and stepped outside.

"Bodie."

"Benteen." Bodie indicated the second

141

man. "This the feller you told me about?"

"Yeah," Benteen nodded. "Will Jordan."

Jordan, a slight, pale-haired man with frosty blue eyes, nodded briefly.

"Will here ain't much for talkin'," Benteen said. "But he'll be there come the day."

"You told him what the job is?" Bodie asked.

"Yeah, an' he's interested." Benteen scratched his jaw. "That herd we brung in . . . well, she weren't big and the money wasn't much . . . "

Bodie recalled the way Benteen had counted his cash in the saloon before buying his drink. "The pay on this job is good," he stressed. "If things start to happen you'll probably have to fight for every damn dollar."

"You want us to start tonight?" Benteen asked.

Bodie nodded. "I'll fetch my horse and take you up to the mine. Show you round."

Shortly they were riding up the rutted trail, the daylight fading around them. With the setting sun casting an orange glow over the earth and black shadows creeping out to meet them, Bodie could have been forgiven for thinking that everything was peaceful. But he knew that appearances could be deceptive. His instincts warned him to stay on his guard. It was a long time to dawn and anything could happen during the dark hours of night . . .

10

AFTER his meeting with Angela Crown and the man called Bodie, Jonas Randall had carried on back to High Grade. On reaching town he had driven the buckboard to his company offices and had gone inside, making his way to his private office on the second floor, overlooking the main street. There were two telegraph messages waiting on his desk. Randall read the first casually, then screwed it up and tossed it aside. He took the second message and scanned it quickly. A hard look came into his eyes and his handsome face darkened with anger. He sat down behind his desk and re-read the telegraph message. This time he read it slowly, digesting every word with care. And then he placed the message on the desk, swivelling his chair to face the window. He remained in that position for a long time, deep in thought.

Abruptly Randall rose to his feet. He strode across the office and yanked open the door.

"Hicks!" he bawled across the outer office. "Get in here fast!"

By the time Randall had sat down again the man called Hicks was standing before his desk.

"I want you to go and find Captain Deeks," Randall said, his voice too loud. "Tell him I want him here now!"

"Yes, Mr Randall," Hicks murmured.

"Hicks, you damn well tell him I mean now — not later. Or tomorrow. I don't care what he's doing! I want him here!"

Ten minutes later Deeks strolled into the office, closing the door at Randall's request. Deeks crossed the room and sat down. He didn't take off his hat because he had become self-conscious about everybody staring at the swathe of white bandage covering his skull.

"Somethin' wrong?" he asked, wondering what had put Randall in such a foul mood.

"Damn right," Randall said. He thrust the telegraph message at Deeks.

Deeks read the message. "Yeah?"

Randall snatched the message back. "You have read it?"

"Yeah! Hell, you was watchin' me. So I read it. And?"

"You understand what it means?"

Deeks shrugged. "Some crap from New York about the Crown mine."

"Judas Priest!" Randall groaned. "Deeks, what you've just read is as near to a sentence of death you'll ever get that doesn't say it in so many words."

"Cut out the fancy crap, Jonas," Deeks said. "Just tell me what it all means."

Randall leaned back in his chair. "In words you can understand, Deeks, that message makes it painfully clear that if we don't complete the purchase of the Crown mines by the end of the month, then we can consider ourselves dead and buried."

Deeks' chair creaked as he moved his heavy bulk. "Balls! They're just trying to hustle us along. Shaking the big stick. Hell, Jonas, they're all the same. They got to keep reminding us they're the big boys."

Frustration showed itself in Randall's eyes as he thrust himself forward, driving a hard fist down on the polished surface of the desk top. "For God's sake, Deeks, listen to me! I've worked for these people for too long. I've seen what can happen to someone who doesn't come through for them. They don't play games, Deeks, and they don't have to show they're the big boys. There's no doubt. Deeks, believe me, they mean business! You don't realise just how big an organisation they are. Back east they have a finger in every damn pie. And I mean everything, from brothels right up to shipbuilding companies. If it makes money they want in. It doesn't matter who owns what.

They find a way to get in, and once they do there's no letting go as long as the money keeps flowing. Right now they see a very big profit in copper. Especially the copper in this mountain. But they won't be satisfied with a little. They want it all, Deeks. Every last little piece."

Deeks scratched his jaw, fingers rasping against unshaven flesh. "Why do they need it all?"

"Because if they get their hands on the whole mountain they can control the selling price. They can negotiate. Push up the price. Alter the stock-market values."

"So why are they getting so fussy all of a sudden?"

"The Government will be issuing contracts next month to companies who can show they have a solid potential for long-term production. The bigger a company is the better contract it'll get. So the more companies we can buy up and have registered before the end of the month the safer we'll be."

Deeks thought over Randall's words for a time. "So what do we do?" he asked finally.

"Concentrate on the Crown mine, Deeks. Increase the pressure. We need that company bad. Every other mine owner in High Grade is watching how Crown behaves. It's the biggest producer on this mountain. If Crown sells out to us the rest will do the same . . . so hit 'em, Deeks, hit 'em hard! I want that company on its knees begging me to buy!"

"What about that son of a bitch Bodie?"

"Angela Crown made a smart move there," Randall said, a mirthless smile crossing his face. "Bodie's already cost us three good men. Oh, by the way, I had a message from Struthers and Cooly. They're in the Ridgelow jail. Bodie put them there."

'Bastard,' Deeks mouthed silently. To Randall: "What are you doin' about them?"

"Struthers and Cooly?" Randall

grinned. "Not a damn thing, Deeks. As far as I'm concerned they can stay in jail and rot."

"I kept telling you that pair were useless," Deeks said. He stood up. "This Bodie!" You want him out of the way?"

"He'll be a damn nuisance as long as he's alive," Randall said. "Though I'd like to have another talk with him. See if I can persuade him he's wasting his time working for Crown."

"I wouldn't mind getting the bastard behind bars myself for a spell," Deeks said. "I owe that son of a bitch!"

"See what you can arrange," Randall suggested.

"It'll be a pleasure," Deeks growled.

Randall watched Deeks carefully adjust his hat. "Just take things easy, Deeks," he said dryly. "Don't let this matter of Bodie go to your head!"

Deeks left the office, banging the door behind him.

For a time Randall remained in his chair. He took a cigar from a box on the desk and lit it. He stood up and went to the window. The daylight was beginning to fade. Lamps were being lit against the approaching darkness. Randall raised his eyes to the dark, looming bulk of the mountain. All that potential wealth, he thought. Enough of it to last for years. If he could pull off the purchase of all the mineral rights it would be worth millions to the people he worked for. And it would set him up for life. Prove his worth in their eyes. He thought of Angela Crown. Her stubborn refusal to sell, even in the face of personal danger. Damn and blast the woman! It wasn't right that one damn woman should stand between him and the greatest triumph of his life. He had to break her. No matter that she was a woman. She'd chosen a man's world so let her play by their rules, hard as they could be. One way or another he would break her. He had to. Because if he didn't break her the organisation would break him. And they were pitiless in their dealings with failed employees. It was no use trying to run from them. Escape was impossible. There was no way out.

Turning from the window Randall picked up his hat and left the office. He made his way through the building, out on to the street. Threading his way along the crowded boardwalk he reached and entered the telegraph office. Nodding curtly to the operator, Randall drew a message pad towards him, and began to write a confident-sounding reply to the message he'd received from his superiors. If he could convince them that he had everything under control they might not bother to send out one of their people to check on him. That was the last thing Randall needed. He had three weeks before the end of the month. If he wasn't able to secure the Crown mine before then nobody would do it. The trouble was, the more he thought about it, the time left to him seemed negligible. Three weeks! To some it could be a lifetime. As far as Jonas Randall was concerned right at that moment, three weeks was nothing. Sweet damn all! And if he didn't come through as he'd promised those three weeks could easily turn into his last days on earth.

11

SOMETIME near midnight Bodie was taking another walk around the Crown mine compound. It was pretty quiet by this time. Most of the miners had turned in for the night, though a lamp still shone from one of the bunkhouse windows. Crossing the open compound Bodie was aware of how vulnerable the place really was to attack. But then it had been designed as a work area and not an army post.

Soft footsteps caught his attention. Bodie eased his rifle out of the crook of his arm as a dark shape came out of the shadows. Then he relaxed as he recognised Hal Benteen's features.

"Bodie?" Benteen asked and caught the answering nod.

"Trouble?" Bodie asked.

"Could be. I reckon I heard horses coming in up the north corner of the compound. Six, maybe seven of them. Moving real cautious."

"Let's go take a look," Bodie said, and they moved off across the dusty, moonlit compound.

The night exploded in their faces! There was a thunderous blast of sound, followed by a brilliant flash. A great, rolling cloud of dust and smoke rose skywards.

"Judas Priest!" Benteen yelled.

Bodie didn't answer. He was already running in the direction of the explosion, knowing full well that they were going to have a fight on their hands.

The blast had come from the section of the compound Benteen had mentioned. As Bodie rounded the end of a long wagon shed he saw the place where the explosion had torn down the fencing, opening a way into the compound, and through the gap rode a bunch of dark-clad riders. They were yelling like Indians, triggering wild shots from their guns, as they began to spread, breaking apart.

Bodie threw his rifle to his shoulder and shot the nearest rider out of his saddle. The rider described a perfect back somersault before his twisting body slammed to the ground, blood fountaining darkly from the ugly wound in his chest. He half rose to his feet, still clutching his gun, and Bodie put two more bullets in him. The man went down a second time, and this time he stayed down.

Pulling back against the wagon shed Bodie let the rest of the riders sweep on by him. Then he stepped out from the blackness and opened fire on the riders. A horse went down, screaming wildly, the rider spinning helplessly across the compound, exposed by the silvery light of the moon. He caught his balance, began to turn, looking for his horse, and found himself face to face with Hal Benteen. There was no hesitation in Benteen's reactions. He simply lifted his handgun and blasted twin holes in the man's chest.

The other riders, realising that things

weren't turning out as they had planned, reined their horses about and began to trade shots with Bodie and Benteen. But the riders were bunched together in the middle of the open compound, illuminated by the moonlight, while Bodie and Benteen, now joined by Will Jordan, were doing their shooting from the shadows.

The compound echoed to the sound of shots, the scream of injured and frightened horses. Bullets howled viciously back and forth.

One of the riders suddenly turned his horse and took it across the compound. Bodie watched him, wondering what the man was up to. The reason revealed itself when the rider jerked his right arm up and forward, tossing something in the direction of the bunkhouse.

Realisation hit Bodie with the force of a physical blow. He ran out from his position beside the wagon shed, across the compound, ignoring the bullets coming his way. Yet even as he ran he knew he was far too late. There wasn't a thing he could do . . .

For the second time the darkness was lit by the flash of an explosion. The dull blast of sound sent shock waves rippling across the compound, and the air was suddenly full of flying debris.

The explosion ripped the bunkhouse wide open. The wooden structure disintegrated under the tremendous force. A billowing pall of smoke engulfed the shattered building. Then, as the smoke subsided, Bodie saw the orange tongues of flame rising out of the great, tangled mass of splintered wood.

A wild rage flowed over Bodie. Heedless of his own danger he angled across the compound, his rifle blasting shot after shot at the assembled riders. From the other direction Benteen and Jordan were doing the same. The riders found themselves caught in a deadly crossfire. Two went down. Then a third. A panic set in amongst the riders. As if with a single thought they turned their horses, spurring them back across the compound, towards the gap in the fencing. Bodie, Benteen and Jordan followed them, emptying two more saddles before the remaining riders went through the fence and on into the shrouding darkness beyond.

"Jordan!" Bodie yelled. "Stay close. Keep your eye on that gap! If anything shows in that hole, put a bullet in it!"

Jordan, already reloading his rifle, nodded, and walked in the direction of the shattered fence.

"Hell, Bodie, I know you said things might get lively," Benteen remarked as they walked back towards the bunkhouse. He thumbed back his hat, surveying the destruction before him. "Lively ain't the goddam word!"

Dazed figures, bloody and heat-scorched, were stumbling from the wreckage of the bunkhouse. From the pile of shattered timber could be heard the moans of injured men, and somewhere a man was crying out in pain.

Bodie and Benteen put aside their rifles and moved to help the men coming out of the debris. One of the first Bodie encountered was Len Treval. The mine manager had a bad gash over his left eye that was spilling blood down his face. He was clutching at his left arm, and Bodie saw that there was a thick sliver of wood deeply embedded in the upper part of the arm. Despite his injuries Treval was fully in control of his senses.

"You get any of them, Bodie?" he asked.

Bodie nodded. "Yeah."

"Good!" Treval hissed through clenched teeth. He glared up at Bodie. "If you find any of the bastards still alive let me know!" You hear me, Bodie?"

"I hear you, Treval, and I reckon half of High Grade can as well. Now go and sit down somewhere until I can get the doctor up here."

"Hey, Bodie, you want me to go and fetch him?" Benteen asked.

"Do that, Benteen, Tell him what's happened and say we aren't sure yet how bad it is."

Benteen turned and ran to his horse. He opened the main gates of the compound and rode off down the trail in the direction of High Grade.

Bodie spent the next half-hour doing what he could for the survivors of the explosion. By the time Benteen returned with the doctor and Angela Crown, Bodie had made a count of the miners. There were four dead. Three had serious wounds from the explosion. The rest, including Len Treval, had escaped with relatively minor wounds. Bodie had also checked the shot raiders. Here the mortality rate proved higher. There were seven dead and three wounded.

"Bodie, I can't believe it," Angela said. Her eyes were moist with tears as she moved among the dead and wounded. "Is this really happening? Is Randall so desperate to get his hands on this mine he condones this sort of thing?"

"Looks that way," Bodie muttered. "You ready to quit?"

Angela looked at him in amazement. "Are you being funny, Bodie?"

"No. But this is as good a time as any to step back and figure the odds. Hell, Angela, it ain't going to get any better."

She sighed wearily. "No, I realise that, Bodie." Then: "But I'm damned if I'll be intimidated! Let Randall do his worst! The Crown mine is not for sale!"

"Maybe it's time we played by Randall's rules," Bodie said, and crossed over to where Len Treval sat waiting for the doctor to get round to him. He glanced up as Bodie approached. "Treval, you got any explosives on the site?"

"Sure," Treval said. "But what the hell do you want . . ." A gleam showed in his eyes. "Bodie, what are you up to?"

"This mess started with a bang tonight," Bodie said. "I figure it ought to end with one."

Treval showed the manhunter the small hut where the explosives were stored. He watched as Bodie helped himself to some sticks and fuses.

"You go easy with that stuff, Bodie," the Cornishman said. "Hell, man, I don't want you blowin' yourself to hell and back!"

"Treval, calm down. I've played with this stuff before."

Bodie crossed to his tethered horse and swung up into the saddle. As he began to move off Angela appeared at his side.

"Where are you going, Bodie?" she asked.

Bodie smiled down at her. "Something I got to do," he said. "You look after things here. I'll see you later."

"Bodie, you be careful!" Angela called as he rode off.

Once he was out of sight of the mine Bodie left the trail and took his horse across country. There were a number of curious sightseers on the trail, all moving in the direction of the Crown mine and Bodie didn't want any contact with them. He rode at a steady pace, entering High Grade from the darkness at the rear of the main street. He found a place where he could tether his horse out of sight and made his way on foot along the silent backyards of the buildings.

He eventually reached his destination and spent some time checking that the building was empty before he forced a rear window, slipping silently inside. He located the stairs leading to the upper floor, and on the landing he paused, kneeling on the floor while he prepared the sticks of explosives he'd brought with him. His preparations completed, Bodie set the bundle of the floor, struck a match, and lit the fuse. It would take about twelve minutes for it to burn down, enough time for Bodie to leave the building, collect his horse, and go find himself a place where he could watch the result of his handiwork in comfort.

Five minutes later Bodie was tethering his horse to the hitch rail of a saloon. He stepped inside the noisy room, elbowing his way to the bar and ordered a drink. Nobody paid him any attention. Bodie leaned against the bar and enjoyed the momentary relaxation.

When the explosion came it caught Bodie unaware. The heavy blast of sound filled the saloon. An orange glare lit up the painted windows. Something flew across the street and shattered one of the windows, showering glass into the saloon. Men began to shout. A woman screamed. And then there was a mad stampede for the door as everyone went to have a look.

Bodie was suddenly alone at the bar. He glanced at the bartender who was stolidly wiping the top of the bar with a damp cloth.

"You hear something?" Bodie asked.

The bartender shook his head. "I don't hear nothin', mister," he said.

"That way I don't get trouble."

Bodie smiled at the man's wisdom. He tossed some money on the bar and strolled to the door. A skinny man with wide eyes pushed past him, grinning all over his face.

"You hear what happened?" he asked Bodie, dying to tell someone what had taken place.

"What?" Bodie asked.

"Some son of a bitch went and blew Jonas Randall's office building to matchwood!" The man giggled excitedly. "Hell, Randall's goin' to be mad as a wet hen when he finds out what happened.

Bodie shoved his way through the crowd outside the saloon. He untied his horse and climbed into the saddle, turning the animal up the street. He glanced at Randall's building as he rode by. The whole place was gutted, flames rising skywards from the tangled debris. Bright sparks floated off in the blackness, glowing briefly before they faded away.

Bodie rode on, out of High Grade, back towards the Crown mines. The line of sightseers, who had left town to investigate the explosion at the Crown mine, were now making the return journey to have a look at the night's second strange occurrence. Bodie rode by them without so much as a glance. He was deep in thought, trying to figure Randall's response to the strike back at him. The man wouldn't let it go. Sometime, somewhere, he would hit out. Bodie knew he was going to have to be ready. Randall didn't play games. He meant every move he made to have the maximum effect.

Bodie didn't mind that. It was the way he played all the time. It was why he was still alive. And he intended to stay in that condition for a long time yet.

12

"**B**ODIE!" Angela's voice was low, softly inviting.

He glanced at her, conscious of his tiredness. "Yeah?"

"Don't be long!" It was as much a plea as it was a directive, and its meaning wasn't lost on Bodie.

He watched Angela vanish inside the house. He took the reins of their horses and led them across the yard at the rear of the house, pushing open the door of the stable. Taking the animals inside he led them to separate stalls, tethered them, then unsaddled and fed them. He tidied away the saddles and trappings, bent to pick up his rifle and gear, and that was when the world exploded around him.

The blow might have killed a lesser man. The force behind it, slamming down between Bodie's shoulders, hurled him across the shadowed stable. He smashed into the plank wall, spinning off it to fall face down on the dirt floor. He lay stunned. For long seconds he was utterly helpless. Then life began to drift slowly back into his numbed mind, and Bodie's survival reflexes took over.

Out of the corner of his eye he caught sight of a huge shadow moving across the stable floor. His attacker moved on silent feet, lightly for such a big man. But light or not he was almost up to Bodie, and that left him hardly any time at all.

Bodie rolled, twisting over onto his back. And looked up into the scarred, brutal face of Beth Arling's mulatto bodyguard — Mantee. Seeing the mulatto's huge, powerful frame, Bodie realised he would be in trouble if he didn't do something quickly, and something positive.

His right hand slid down to the heavy Colt holstered on his hip, fingers closing over the butt. Bodie lifted the gun, easing back the hammer. Yet before the Colt was levelled Mantee had lunged forward, his left hand sweeping round in a brutal curve. He caught hold of Bodie's gunhand, twisting cruelly. The gun slid from Bodie's fingers, slithering off into the shadows. Still holding Bodie's gunhand Mantee yanked him off the ground, pulling the manhunter towards him. Bodie sensed Mantee's intention. He knew he couldn't allow himself to be encirlced by Mantee's huge arms.

Bodie allowed Mantee to pull him close, then just before the mulatto swept both arms around his body, Bodie reached down and closed his fingers over the handle of his sheathed knife. Slipping it free he brought it up from his left side, the blade glittering in the early light. The blade cut through Mantee's shirt and sank into the flesh of his right side. Hot blood spurted from the wound as Bodie shoved hard, twisting the knife as it penetrated deep. Mantee grunted. His right hand lashed out, catching Bodie across the side of the head, a solid blow that knocked Bodie back across the stable. Mantee, the knife still protruding from his side, lumbered across the stable. His great hands reached out and caught hold of Bodie's shirt. He swung Bodie with all the ease of a child lifting a doll, releasing him at the apex of the swing. Bodie was literally thrown across the stable. He was brought up short by the wall again, his body bursting with pain. Dragging his feet under him Bodie lurched upright, ducking beneath Mantee's lunging fists. Bodie drove a hard right into Mantee's stomach. The mulatto grunted and hammered his fist down across the back of Bodie's neck, spilling him to the floor again. Before Bodie could react Mantee had bent over him, his huge hands closing around Bodie's neck. Mantee dug in his thick fingers and began to squeeze. Almost immediately Bodie began to choke. The pressure on his neck was tremendous. He couldn't breathe and he knew it wouldn't be long before he blacked out. He thrust out his right arm, fingers groping the air, seeking something, anything he could use as a weapon. At first there was nothing. Then Bodie's fingers brushed something hard. He reached again and closed his fingers around the object. It took precious seconds for him to realise what it was. He had hold of the handle of his knife, still jammed in Mantee's body. The handle was slick with blood. Bodie gripped the handle tight and yanked. The blade slid free from Mantee's body, drawing a spurt of blood. The moment he had the knife in his hand Bodie thrust the upturned blade above his head. He was hoping desperately that the blade might find the vulnerable flesh of Mantee's throat. It was a wild hope, but it was all Bodie had. He thrust and kept thrusting, jabbing at the unseen, empty air above his head, not knowing how near or now far he might be from his intended target.

And then the keen blade struck something solid. Bodie struck again, putting all his remaining strength into the blow. There was a soft, moist sound, the knife sinking into something fleshy. A deep, shuddering moan burst from Mantee's lips. A hot wetness dribbled down the side of Bodie's face. And Mantee's hands were drawn away from his neck. Bodie lunged forward, dragging his feet under him, struggling to draw air back into his starved lungs. He could hear Mantee behind him moaning softly like some hurt animal, stumbling about across the stable floor.

Pulling himself upright by one of the stall posts Bodie turned, his eyes seeking Mantee. The mulatto was in the centre of the stable, on his knes, his hands raised to his face. Mantee's hands and arms were covered in blood. So was his face. The blood was oozing heavily from around the blade of Bodie's knife, which was buried deeply in the mulatto's right eye socket. The razor-like blade had penetrated Mantee's eyeball, destroying it completely, slicing its way into the inner cavity. As Bodie turned in his direction Mantee closed his hands over the handle of the knife and yanked it out of his flesh. A gout of blood erupted from the wound.

Mantee stared at Bodie with his good eye. He seemed to be grinning through the bloody mess covering his face. He held up the knife and began to move down the stable.

Bodie backed off. He drew level with the stall he'd used for his horse. The horse was busy with the feed Bodie had forked into the trough only minutes before. It paid no attention to what was going on around it.

Damn! The pitchfork! Where the hell had he put it? Bodie backed up against the next stall. He heard something slither along the wooden partition and out of the corner of his eye he saw the long handle of the two-pronged pitchfork, disturbed by his contact with the stall, sliding towards the floor.

Bodie threw a swift glance in Mantee's direction. He saw the mulatto pause, head cocked to one side, and then, as if anticipating Bodie's thoughts, Mantee lunged forward, knife held before him, slashing at Bodie's body.

Bodie turned in at the stall, dropping to one knee, hands reaching for the pitchfork. He took hold, began to turn, bringing the two shiny prongs up in a glittering arc. He sensed Mantee's huge bulk rearing over him, the mutilated face red with blood, and then he thrust the pitchfork up at his body.

The prongs ripped deep into Mantee's taut throat, one bursting out of the back of his neck. The moment he felt the prongs penetrate Bodie began to push, driving Mantee back, shoving hard. Mantee fought the terrible push of the cold metal buried deep in his flesh. Then he was pushed into a corner of an empty stall, and there was nowhere else to go. He dropped the knife and curled his fingers round the handle of the pitchfork, desperately trying to remove the offending prongs from his throat. He began to twist and jerk his great body from side to side, but all he managed to do was to worsen the effect of the prongs. The edge of one prong severed the main artery and blood began to spurt from the wound in his throat.

Bodie let go of the pitchfork. He moved away from Mantee. The man was as good as dead. Searching the stable floor Bodie found his gun. Checking it he put it away.

He caught a slight sound by the stable door and turned. It was Angela. She came into the stable, her tired face registering shock when she saw the state he was in.

"Bodie . . . what's happened?" she asked, and then her gaze was drawn to the silently struggling figure of Mantee, locked in his death throes. "Oh . . . God . . . Bodie!"

"He was waiting for me," Bodie said. "You know who he is?"

Angela was silent for a time. "Yes, I know who he is."

"Well?"

"He's called Mantee. He is a bodyguard. For . . . for Beth Arling!"

Bodie didn't say a word. He scooped up his hat from the floor and made for the door.

"Bodie, where are you going?" Angela asked, knowing the worst was still to come.

"I'm going to see a lady about a mulatto!" Bodie snapped.

"Bodie . . . please!" Angela called.

He stopped, looked back over his shoulder. "Angela, something stinks about all this! I'm going to find out what."

"I'm sure Raymond isn't mixed up in it."

Bodie's stare was bleak. "The hell you're sure!" he said, and turned away.

He walked away from the house. He hated having to do it, because he knew that the truth, if it happened to be the truth he expected, was going to hurt Angela badly. But there was no nice way round it. If Angela's brother was mixed up in some scheme, and Bodie was damn sure now that he was, then there was no way she could be protected from that fact.

He made his way down the hill towards High Grade. The sun was barely showing over the horizon. If the rest of the day went the way it had started, Bodie figured it might have been better to have stayed in bed.

13

AT this early hour High Grade was pretty well deserted. A few stragglers were weaving their way home — or to whatever constituted home. In one or two windows lamplight gleamed, either from latecomers just going to bed, or from early risers. High Grade lay silent, locked in that drawn-out time which is neither night or day.

Bodie paused outside the saloon, his eyes raking the shadowed windows on the upper floor. This was the place. The sign over the boardwalk porch said it all: THE ARLING PALACE. It was the saloon he'd been in the day before. Where he had met and hired Hal Benteen. And where, on his way out, he had realised that he was being watched. A young woman with blonde hair standing at the balcony rail. Behind her two men, in the shadows. Figures he hadn't been able to identify then. But now Bodie was sure. Sure that one of those men had been the mulatto, the man called Mantee. And that the other had been Angela's brother. Raymond Crown.

He stepped up onto the boardwalk and pushed in through the swing doors, his boots echoing on the plank floor. The saloon was empty, most of the lamps turned down. The room looked bigger now, cold and almost bleak.

A faint sound caught Bodie's attention and he glanced across the saloon. Behind the bar stood a lonely figure. A bartender, half-asleep, resignedly wiping the top of the bar, clearing away the spillages of the night's business.

"We're closed," he said sullenly, not even looking up at Bodie's approach.

"I didn't come looking for a drink," Bodie told him.

Something in his tone made the bartender raise his head. He stared at Bodie, noting the fresh bruises on the manhunter's face.

"If you want doctoring you chose the wrong door, mister!"

"Keep up the smart talk, feller, and you'll be the one needing the doctor," Bodie said. "Now just tell me which is Beth Arling's room and we'll part company on a friendly basis."

The bartender put down the glass he was wiping. He carefully folded the cloth in his hands and placed it beside the glass.

"The boss don't like being disturbed, he said. 'Especially at this time of day."

"I don't give a damn what she doesn't like," Bodie snapped. "And I ain't too bothered whether you tell me where she is. I'll find her even if I have to kick down every door in this place!"

The bartender's face stiffened. "One of the tough ones, huh?" he muttered, his left hand reaching under the bar, starting to lift out the loaded, sawn-off shotgun he kept there for just this kind of occasion.

"No," Bodie said in reply. "Just the toughest!"

His right hand snaked across the bar as the black muzzles of the shotgun appeared. Powerful fingers knotted themselves in the loose front of the bartender's shirt. Bodie dragged the man halfway across the bar, driving his left fist full into the bartender's surprised face. The sound of the blow was loud in the empty saloon. The bartender gave a stunned gasp as his lips were smashed back against his teeth, blood welling from torn flesh and gums. His eyes glazed over and he lost interest in the entire episode. Bodie snatched the shotgun from his hand, shoving the bartender away from him. The man sagged back against the loaded shelves at the rear of the bar, slithering to the floor in a cascade of dislodged bottles.

Bodie moved away from the bar, heading for the stairs. He broke the shotgun, saw that it was loaded and snapped it shut again. He had almost reached the stairs when a door at the end of the bar opened and a bleary-eyed figure lurched into view.

"What the hell is all the racket about, Ed?"

Bodie swung the shotgun up and jabbed the muzzles against the man's stomach. "Ed's off duty, feller," he said. "Looks like you've been elected."

The man scrubbed at his sleepy eyes. "Who the fuck are you?" he asked.

"You the bouncer in this dump?" Bodie asked, taking in the man's hefty build and the broken-nosed, scarred face.

"Yeah! What's it to you?"

"Just that if you don't tell me what I want to know I'm going to bounce you all the way out of town!"

The bouncer grinned, his lips peeling back to reveal crooked yellow teeth. "Who says so?" he asked.

Bodie reversed the shotgun and smacked the bouncer across the side of the jaw with the butt. The man stumbled back against the wall, cursing softly, pawing at the bloody side of his face.

"Not polite to keep asking questions," Bodie said. "You could get hurt!"

"Son of a goddam bitch," the bouncer grumbled. "What makes you figure you can go round slugging me?"

"That's easy, feller," Bodie told him. "I got the gun. You want to argue some more?"

The bouncer raised a big hand. "Back off," he said. "I ain't that stupid!"

"Make me believe you by telling me where I can find Beth Arling." Bodie suggested.

The bouncer's eyes flicked from Bodie's face to the menacing shape of the shotgun. He ran his tongue over his lips suddenly gone dry.

"What the hell," he said with a shrug. "I can always find another job. Up the stairs. Along the balcony. It's the last door but one."

Bodie nodded. Easy, wasn't it? Just in case you get an attack of conscience, feller, you remember what I'm holding." Bodie raised the shotgun a little. Just enough so that the bouncer got the message.

"Look, mister, I'm paid to throw out customers when they get drunk and cause trouble. The place is closed right now. And you ain't drunk. And as far as I know you ain't caused no trouble. So . . . !"

"So?"

"So I'm goin' back to bed. That's where I'll be for the rest of the day. An' if I'm asleep I can't hear nothin' or see nothing'."

The bouncer backed away from Bodie until he reached the door he had come through minutes before. He went into the room beyond, closing the door firmly. Bodie turned and carried on up the stairs. At the top he turned along the balcony, easing his way to the door the bouncer had described.

He didn't waste time checking to see if the door was locked or not. A well placed boot splintered the wood around the lock. The door flew open with a crash, and Bodie was inside the room before it had struck the inner wall.

He was in a woman's bedroom. It was obvious from the decor and the heady scent of perfume and powder. There was a woman in the big bed. Young and blonde. The same woman Bodie had spotted watching him from the balcony overlooking the saloon. There was a man in the bed beside her. Even on his initial look at the man's face Bodie saw a likeness to Angela Crown.

The woman sat upright as Bodie burst in. She was dazed, her face drugged with sleep, the blonde hair loose and tousled. She was naked under the blankets, Bodie saw, as the bedclothes fell away from her shoulders, exposing her full, well-shaped breasts. For a moment she stared at him, her eyes blank. Then she seemed to snap into life, her gaze sharpening, awareness coming to her in an instant.

"Bodie! What do you want with me?"

Bodie smiled at her confidence. He pushed the door shut, keeping the shotgun trained on the bed as he noticed the man stirring sluggishly.

"I figured it was time we met, honey," he said easily.

Beth Arling watched him intently. She wasn't being fooled by his manner. Bodie waited as she pushed aside the bedclothes and swung her shapely legs to the floor.

"Mr Bodie, you've caught me with my pants down, as the saying goes," she said, rising to her feet, making no attempt to conceal her ripe nudity.

"Never was one for the formal approach." Bodie let his gaze travel from her feet to the top of her blonde head. "You should look good in black," he said.

Beth Arling frowned. "What do I need to wear black for?"

"I figure you'll be going to Mantee's funeral!" Bodie observed.

Beth Arling's face became ugly with shock and rage. For a long moment her whole body tensed, and then with a strangled cry she launched herself at Bodie, long fingernails slashing at his face.

"You killed Mantee!" she screamed.

Bodie eased his body to one side, avoiding her headlong rush, and in the same movement he swept up his left hand, slapping her across the face. The sound of the slap was like a pistol shot. Beth Arling was flung to one side. She lost her balance and sprawled across the carpeted floor in an inelegant tangle of bare arms and legs.

"He wasn't good enough," Bodie said. "So he's dead and I'm here. And I want some straight answers to some plain questions!"

"He's going to kill us!"

Raymond Crown was on his feet, dragging his pants on over his nakedness. He looked like a man who had suddenly found there was no place left to hide.

Bodie strode around the bed and caught hold of Crown's arm. The man yelled in fear as Bodie dragged him to the middle of the room.

"You paid Kopek to kill your sister while she was on her way back from Ridgelow."

Crown stared at him through frightened eyes. Sweat gleamed on the pallid face. A line of spittle trickled from the corner of his mouth.

"You son of a bitch!" Bodie said. He rammed the muzzles of the shotgun into Raymond Crown's naked stomach, feeling the man cringe from the cold steel. "I want an answer from you, mister, or we're all going to find out if you've got any guts inside your carcase!"

"I . . . I . . . for God's sake, man, you can't just kill me!" Crown's voice rose to a shrill wail. "You have to listen . . . to me . . . !"

"That's where you're wrong, feller, I don't!" Bodie snapped. "All I have to do is pull a trigger. What happens after that won't concern you at all!"

"It wasn't my fault!" Crown yelled. He threw an arm in the direction of Beth Arling. "She made me do it! It was her!"

A cold rage grew in Bodie's chest. It drove him to wild, unfeeling action. He shoved Raymond Crown away from him, and as the man stood uncertainly in the centre of the room, Bodie swung a brutal fist into his face. Crown's nose splintered with a sodden crunch, blood spraying from the crushed flesh. Gasping for breath Crown back away, but Bodie followed him across the room, his fist striking again and again. Hard knuckles smashed against soft flesh, pulping lips and breaking teeth from bloody gums. Crown was spun on his heel by a sledging left to his jaw, driving him against the wall. He tried to stay on his feet by clawing at the wall. His battered face left a bloody smear on the faded wallpaper. Crown was weeping uncontrollably, the sound choking off when Bodie sank his fist deep into his side. Crown sank to his knees, clutching his body, retching violently.

Bodie stepped back from the man, angry at himself for allowing his anger to divert his attention from Beth Arling. She was the more dangerous of the two. Even as he registered his mistake he heard a soft sound behind him, a sharp intake of breath, followed by the metallic click of a gun hammer being pulled back.

You damn fool, he yelled to himself, and turned, letting his body drop to the floor.

A gun went off. The sound was sharp, hard, the blast from a light calibre weapon, Bodie registered. Then he hit the floor and rolled frantically as he caught sight of Beth Arling. She was on her feet, legs braced apart, a look of wild triumph on her lovely face as she followed the movement of his body with the gun held in her hands. It fired a second time. The bullet gouged a long tear in the carpet, pale splinters of wood flying up in the air. Beth began to draw back the hammer again. It only took an instant. But in that time Bodie had let go of the shotgun, snatched at his holstered Colt, and fired a single shot. The bullet hit Beth Arling in the soft flesh of her upper arm, spinning her round and dumping her on the floor. Blood streaked the pale flesh of her arm and the rounded fullness of her breasts. She lay in a shocked stupor, her eyes wide, unseeing, and Bodie knew that in a while she would begin to feel the pain.

He climbed to his feet. Picking up the gun Beth Arling had used he tucked it under his belt. Then he went across the room to where Raymond Crown lay. Pulling the man to his feet Bodie shoved him to the bed and sat him on the edge.

"Now we've all played games, feller, let's talk. And this time we have some answers."

Raymond Crown wiped blood from his mouth. "All right," he mumbled.

"What do I care any more!"

"Never mind the hearts and flowers," Bodie said. "Kopek! You hired him?"

"Yes."

"Randall must be offering a hell of a deal to make you go that far. What's his price?"

"A million and a half," Crown whispered hoarsely. He abruptly raised his head and stared at Bodie, a desperate wildness showing in his eyes. "We would have been rich, man! Able to leave this goddamn place. Go where there are civilised people. Restaurants. Theatres. Music. Anywhere away from this filthy mountain! It was wrong. Angela had no right refusing to sell! She had no damn right to keep me here! I don't belong!"

"That's the only thing you're right about, feller," Bodie observed. "You sure as hell don't belong. Not here or anywhere! Only place fit for you is a cage! Now get on your feet and get dressed!"

Bodie picked up the shotgun, tucking

it under his arm. He crossed to where Beth Arling lay and pulled her roughly to her feet. She gazed at him through dull eyes.

"You too, honey," he said.

Beth pulled away from him, her mouth twisting into an ugly sneer. "Big man," she spat. "I hope you burn in hell, Bodie!"

"The way you act, honey, I'll probably have company," Bodie said. "Now get some clothes on, or I'll drag you outside the way you are!"

Ten minutes later they emerged from the saloon to find a sprinkling of High Grade's citizens gathered outside the building. One of those waiting was Angela Crown. As she saw Bodie step out on the boardwalk she pushed her way to the front of the crowd.

"Bodie, are you all right?" she asked.

He nodded. "Ask your brother what he's been up to, Angela."

Angela glanced at her brother, flinching slightly at the sight of his battered, bloody face. "I didn't want to admit the possibility, Raymond. I thought about it and the more I thought, the less I wanted to know. But I'm not a child. I can't avoid the truth. And the truth is that you wanted me . . . dead! Isn't that correct, Raymond?"

"Yes!" Raymond Crown screamed. "Yes, it's true! I wanted you dead and buried! Out of my hair for good! All that money waiting for me and it might as well have been at the bottom of the sea! Because you're so goddam stubborn, you self-righteous bitch!"

Angela's face paled at his vicious outburst. She took a hesitant step forward, and then shrank away, turning on her heel. The gathered crowd melted aside as she moved across the street to where her horse stood.

"No!"

Raymond Crown's hysterical yell shattered the silence. In a sudden lunge he drove his shoulder against Bodie, knocking him back across the boardwalk. In the same movement his fingers closed around the shotgun in Bodie's hand, snatching the deadly weapon free. Turning, Raymond ran down the steps and onto the street, his fingers fumbling with the shotgun's hammers. His face was taut, a bitter mask of unrelenting fury.

The crowd scattered at the sight of the running man and the raised shotgun.

Bodie, recovering his balance, reached for his holstered Colt, dragging back the hammer as the gun came up.

Alarmed by the outburst Angela turned and saw her brother running toward her, the shotgun levelled at her.

Raymond, his finger drawing back on the double trigger, began to smile. A wild, almost insane expression.

A shot rang out. Then another.

Raymond Crown was spun round by the force of the heavy bullets. One took him in the chest, high up, blowing a pulpy hole through his body. Blood and torn flesh spewed from the exit wound. The second shot hit him in the throat, ripping it open in a red spray. Bloody tissue erupted from Raymond's slack mouth as he stumbled to his knees in the dust. His finger jerked on the shotgun's triggers and the weapon blasted its loads into the dirt. With blood pumping from his shattered body Raymond Crown toppled forward, limbs jerking awkwardly as he died.

Bodie came down off the boardwalk, his unfired gun in his fist. As he pushed his way across the street he saw Hal Benteen coming from behind Angela. Benteen's gun was in his hand, smoke curling from the muzzle.

"He didn't give me any choice, Miss Crown," Benteen said apologetically.

Angela nodded. "Thank you, Mr Benteen." She glanced at her brother's body. "He didn't leave any of us with a choice," she said sadly, her eyes misting with tears.

"Angela, let's go back to the house," Bodie said.

"It ain't over yet," Benteen said. "Randall ain't finished . . . and he's goin' to be good and mad with you, Bodie, after last night!"

Bodie smiled wolfishly. "That's just what I'm hoping," he said.

Standing at the edge of the boardwalk Beth Arling watched the street empty. She fixed her gaze on the bloody corpse of Raymond Crown and she knew that her dreams of big money were ended. Maybe she was lucky, though. At least she was still alive. She was aware of how close she'd come to dying. So perhaps it was time for her to leave High Grade. Sell the saloon and move on. There were other towns. Other opportunities. She had made enough money out of High Grade to be able to sell the saloon quickly, even at a loss. And she had enough capital banked away in various accounts to keep her solvent. The only thing she really regretted was the death of Mantee. For that she could never forgive Bodie. And maybe one day, no matter when, she might find herself in the position to repay him for Mantee's death.

It was a thought that would keep her awake at night — but it would be worth every long, lonely, aching minute!

14

"I STILL say let's go and find him," Deeks yelled. He smashed his fist down on the desk top. "Put some lead in the son of a bitch!"

"A man like Bodie doesn't die easy," Jonas Randall said. "I think he's proved that in the short time he's been involved with Angela Crown."

Deeks slumped in his chair, glowering at Randall's back. The worst of it was that Randall was right. All Deeks had to do was to think back to the events of the night before. The raid on the Crown mine had turned out to be extremely costly. Most of Deeks' best guns were dead — or wounded — and the rest of his men were starting to figure the odds. None of them seemed too happy about getting involved with Bodie any more. The abortive raid had been galling enough. Bodie's swift, unexpected reaction — blowing up Randall's office building — had been downright embarrassing. And then there had been the violent showdown between Bodie and Raymond Crown. Even Randall had been surprised at the revelation of Crown's involvement with Beth Arling.

"Damn," Randall said. He was staring out of the window of Deeks' office, and he turned suddenly. "If only Crown had come to me instead of that whore. We could have helped each other without all this mess exploding in our faces."

"You ask me," Deeks observed, "I'd say it was the Arling woman who talked Crown into trying to kill his sister. Crown was a greedy son of a bitch, but he hadn't the brains or the guts to dream up a scheme like that. Hell, he had hot pants for Beth Arling. Everybody knew it. Couldn't keep away from her. All she had to do was show him her tail, give him what he was after, and he would've done anything."

Randall crossed the office. "Maybe you're right, Deeks. God, I could swear at the thought of the chance we missed there!"

"Yeah, well it ain't going to do any good moanin' about it. What we got to do now is make sure that when we go for Bodie there ain't no more foul-ups!"

"I want something done quickly, Deeks. The longer Bodie's around the harder it'll get for us. Every time he hits and hurts us, the rest of High Grade takes notice. Sooner or later they'll all start resisting, and if that happens we can forget about making this a company town and start digging a couple of graves!"

"You want me to try and pick up a few more guns?" Deeks asked.

"If you can. And throw in some more money. That should stop the rest of those miserable bastards grumbling."

Deeks picked up his hat and strode out of the office. He made his way out onto the street. The sun had been up for a few hours now and High Grade boiled in dusty subservience. Deeks glanced up and down the busy street, then began to cross, making his way down to the far end of the main intersection. Down here was the dirty, forgotten part of town. Where the drunks and the layabouts and the cheap whores existed — they didn't live, they existed — drifting from day to day without purpose or plan or ambition. Their indifference towards life was shown by the filthy, ramshackle hovels in which they squandered each day, each hour. The cramped huts were thrown together from old packing cases, the odd length of timber, sacking and canvas. The narrow alleys between were overflowing with filth of all kinds. And the place reeked of humanity at its lowest.

There were men and women down here who would do anything for a couple of dollars. Deeks had a specific couple of people in mind. Twin brothers by the name of Jelks.

Artie and Simm Jelks. They were a pair of vicious, brutal, degenerates. As far as Deeks was concerned, the Jelkses were little more than two-legged animals. But they were just what he needed for the job in hand.

The Jelkses' hut stood on its own, a way off from its neighbours. The two brothers weren't concerned with the rest of High Grade's outcasts. They preferred to be separate. As Deeks got close to the hut he was able to smell the rotting filth strewn around outside the place. Reaching the door he hammered on it.

"Artie? Simm? You boys in there? It's Deeks. I want to talk."

Somebody giggled inside the hut. Bare feet scuttled across the floor and the door was dragged open on its creaking hinges.

A naked girl peered out at Deeks. She couldn't have been more than seventeen. Slim, almost boyish in build, with small, hard breasts, she stared at Deeks with wide, dark eyes.

"It's him," she called over her shoulder.

"Well show the man in," a man yelled.

The girl opened the door and Deeks stepped inside the shaded hut. It reeked of stale sweat and the muskiness of sex. The girl closed the door and trotted past Deeks, her small, round buttocks bouncing tightly. Against the far wall of the hut stood a large old bed. The girl climbed onto the bed and put her arms around the naked man stretched out on the grubby blankets. A second man, naked as well, was kneeling on the bed. He grinned across the room at Deeks.

"Nice to see you, Mr Deeks," he said. "You come on business? Only Simm an' me, well, we's kind of tied up at the present!"

Deeks didn't answer. He was watching what the girl was doing to Simm Jelks' large erection. He had heard about the way some girls would do it with their mouths but this was the first time he'd actually seen it being done. And while the girl busied herself with Simm, his brother Artie moved to the rear of the girl, guiding his own erection between the spread thighs. He lunged forward with a deep grunt, mounting her as a stallion would a mare. Deeks stood and watched, fascinated by the animal-like lust of the straining trio on the swaying bed. He was aware of his own partial arousal, but he didn't move until the three on the bed were finished.

Artie Jelks, grinning all over his lean, unshaven face, climbed off the bed and picked up a pair of filthy Levis. He pulled them on, then got down on hands and knees, searching under the bed until he located a pair of scuffed boots. He squatted on the floor while he tugged the boots on over his dirty feet, then climbed upright to stamp his feet firmly down into the tight leather.

"Ain't seen you in a coon's age, Deeks," Artie said finally. "Been hearin' 'bout all your troubles, mind."

"Yeah," called Simm from the bed. "Seems to me somebody's givin' you the old run around, Deeks."

Deeks grunted and crossed over to where a pot of coffee stood bubbling on an old pot-bellied stove. He found a reasonably clean mug and poured himself some of the brew. In spite of their appearance the Jelks boys brewed the best coffee Deeks has ever tasted.

Aware of his reluctance to talk, Simm Jelks sat up, gently stroking the girl's taut buttocks. "Hey, Jolene, why don't you come back later? When me an' Artie got time to spare."

The girl sat up. She glared across the room at Deeks. "Aw, I was just gettin' all warmed up too!"

Artie gathered up the girl's dress and tossed it to her. "Well you just wrap a blanket round it, honey, an' keep it warm." He giggled softly, rubbing his hand up and down his groin.

Jolene pulled on her dress. She went to the door, still glaring at Deeks. "I'll see you boys later," she said and slipped out through the door.

"That Jolene!" Artie crooned.

Simm, perched on the end of the bed, was fondling himself. "Man, can that girl do it! She sucked my pecker drier than a water pump in a drought!"

"Time we talked, Deeks," Artie said. He helped himself to coffee.

"I got a job for you boys," Deeks said. "Feller called Bodie."

"We was kinda hoping for a chance at him," Simm said. He was dragging the bedclothes apart as he searched for his clothes.

"Hell, yeah," Artie agreed. "Mean son of a bitch, that Bodie! No offence, Deeks, but he sure took your boys apart!"

"You don't have to tell me," Deeks growled. "If I'd had him workin' for me, this town would've been in Randall's pocket by now." He refilled his coffee mug. "Reckon you can take him?"

Simm, dragging on his pants, chuckled. "We'll take him — or get our asses shot off with the doin'!"

"Deeks, you leave it to us," Artie said.

"While you're at it, I want that Crown woman scared so bad she'll sell out to Randall for the change in his pocket!"

"Now that could be fun," Artie giggled. "Hey, Deeks, I figure this job should be worth a nice little pile."

"You pull it off, boys, and you won't have to stay in this dump any longer."

Simm pulled a face. "Why not? hell, Deeks, we like it here. It's home and it's just fine. Ain't it, Artie?"

"Damn right! We just wouldn't feel right anywhere else, Deeks. An' anyhow, lil' ol' Jolene lives just across the way, an' that gal as got tricks we ain't even tried yet!"

"Get it done then," Deeks said. "You know where to find me after. I'll have cash money ready for you!"

"That's what we want to hear, Deeks." Artie scratched his groin.

"Simm, you got an itch?"

"No, why?"

"I have! Judas Priest, I hope Jolene ain't been passin' anythin' on. It's the only trouble with that little gal. She's so damn generous. If she got a dose of the clap she'd just naturally pass it on so nobody could accuse her of hoggin' it all herself!"

15

ALL through the long day Bodie was aware of tension building up inside him. There was no tangible cause for his mood. No outward threat had shown itself. But he just knew that something was brewing, and it was going to boil over without warning.

Jonas Randall was keeping out of sight, which worried Bodie. Also, Randall's men, including Deeks, had slipped out of sight. Bodie would have given a lot to have known just what they were up to. After all the recent activity, the sudden calm was unnatural.

Late afternoon found Bodie on his way back to High Grade from the Crown mine. Len Treval had worked wonders in the short time since the previous night's raid. He already had men working on the damaged fence and the wrecked bunkhouse. And he was still keeping the mine's production at its normal capacity.

On the surface he had nothing to worry about. Everything seemed normal. Which was why Bodie had a bad feeling.

His feelings heightened his natural senses, and Bodie rode the dust trail towards town in anticipation of trouble.

So when he caught the merest glimpse of sunlight bouncing off some metallic object in the deep brush edging the trail, he reacted instantly, hauling back on the reins and bringing his horse to a complete halt.

Which meant that instead of the burst of spreading shot from a scattergun hitting its intended target, Bodie's horse was struck. The charge hit the animal in the neck, ripping open a pulpy wound that spurted blood. The horse shrieked as it went down, legs thrashing wildly. Before it had struck the ground Bodie was out of the saddle, his hand snatching his Colt free. He hit the ground on his shoulder, letting his forward momentum carry him over the edge of the trail. He crashed into and through the thick brush, ignoring the thorny vegetation. Dust rose in pale clouds, marking his descent, but Bodie wasn't too concerned about giving away his position. He wanted whoever had shot at him to come looking.

He hit the bottom of the slope, coming to his feet, aware of someone moving through the tangled brush. Whoever it was, he thought, had done this kind of thing before. The man moved fast and didn't make much noise. He managed to slide through the dense, brittle undergrowth without disturbing it too much.

Bodie eased back the Colt's hammer, sinking into the shadows at the base of a high rock, and waited.

A silence descended. The ambusher was holding his position. Maybe, like Bodie, he was waiting and listening.

There was a faint whisper of sound at Bodie's rear. The manhunter turned his head slightly. He knew damn well that the ambusher hadn't got behind him. For one thing there hadn't been enough time. So that meant two of them. Bodie smiled. They had planned it carefully. The first one had let Bodie ride by, giving the second man time for his shot. In the case of the shot not killing Bodie it meant they had him between them. All they had to do was close in and take him when they were sure.

Not that Bodie intended to make it that easy for them.

If there was any waiting to be done Bodie was a past master at the art. He'd learned it from experience, back when he'd been seventeen, fighting the Apache in their own country, and there was no better way of learning than that. Providing you survived the course.

The sun continued on its downward slide. The shadows grew and deepened. Bodie was content to wait it out. The darkness held no problems for him. But it apparently bothered his ambushers.

The one behind Bodie began to worm his way forward. He had the same skills as the other, and Bodie acknowledged the man's expertise. But only to a point. As good as he was the man still made too much noise. And it didn't take Bodie too long to spot him. He waited until the man raised himself off the ground, coming to his knees. A gun shone dully in the fading light and behind it Bodie made out the dark outline of a man's body.

He swung the Colt up and triggered two fast shots at the shape.

An unearthly howl of pain followed the blast of gunfire. Bodie's target lurched to his feet, plunging out of the brush, seeming to run directly at Bodie. As Bodie turned towards the man he caught a fleeting glimpse of wild eyes and a mouth thrown wide open in a scream of ragged pain. There was blood too, spurting from the two ragged holes in the man's chest, soaking the filthy shirt, spilling through the skinny fingers the man pressed over the holes. The man weaved as he ran, throwing up the gun he was holding, and began to pull the trigger. Bullets slapped the rock beside Bodie, howling off into the red sky.

Bodie ducked low, tilting up his Colt, firing into the lean body. He saw his bullets hit, saw the flesh burst open in bloody gouts, yet the man still came on, still yelling and firing.

Go down, you son of a bitch, Bodie cursed, and raised the Colt, aware that he was using his last shot. He touched the trigger and the heavy gun slapped his palm in recoil.

The bullet drilled in just below the nose, caving in the front of the face as it flattened against bone. Fragmented bone and lead tore up through the skull cavity, blood spurting from the shattered mouth. The man ran on for half a dozen more steps before the limbs ceased to function and then the thing, which was already a corpse, simply crashed to the ground.

On his feet Bodie circled the high

rock he'd been using, his fingers busy ejecting spent casings from the Colt's cylinder. He could hear the crackle of brush, and knew that the second man was on the move.

So come and get yours, feller! Bodie almost yelled the thought out loud as he thumbed in the final load, snapping back the hammer in readiness.

He heard the man's sudden curse. Bodie realised he had found his dead partner. He angled through the brush, moving along a course that would bring him out behind the ambusher. Which seemed a fair way of doing it, Bodie decided. It was the way they had started the fight . . . and now it would be the way he'd end it.

The lean figure was standing over the dead man, cradling a scattergun in his hands. He was no more than ten feet from Bodie as the manhunter stepped out from the tangled brush, and Bodie saw him tense, slim shoulders lifting.

"Here I am, feller!" Bodie said softly,

and he began to fire even as the man lunged to one side.

Bodie's first shot took the man in the left side, flipping his lean body over, blood jetting from the raw wound. The man hit the ground, rolling lightly, almost making it to his feet. But Bodie's second bullet ripped away his left kneecap in a welter of blood and bone. The man flopped back on the ground, his lips peeling back from his teeth in a savage snarl of anger. He managed to jerk the scattergun in Bodie's direction, touching the trigger. The shotgun howled loudly blasting its deadly charge in a cloud of powdersmoke. Bodie felt the stinging cut of shot rip across the left side, over the ribs, and felt the onrush of blood from lacerated flesh. He triggered shots in return, saw the man on the ground jerk and twitch as bullets ripped away more of his life. The scattergun slipped from weakening fingers. The man tried to pull the gun holstered on his hip, but Bodie reached him before then. He drove the toe of his boot against the man's gun hand. Bone cracked and the gun spun away into the shadows.

"I told Deeks we'd get you or have our asses shot off," Simm Jelks said through a bloody froth.

"You had your chance," Boldie told him. "I'll tell Deeks you wasted your time. Not that he's got much left himself."

Simm managed a slight grin. "Deeks, now, he'll go down fightin'!"

"Feller, I don't give a damn if he goes down singing 'God Bless America', long as he don't get up again!"

"Bodie!"

"Yeah?"

Simm coughed up more blood, groaning against the terrible pain in his chest. "You a tidy kind of feller? Who don't leave a job unfinished?"

"I guess," Bodie said, easing back the Colt's hammer, and putting his last bullet through Simm Jelks' head.

He turned in the direction of High Grade, figuring that if he was going to tidy he might as well sweep away the rest of the town's horsehit!

16

IT was starting to get dark by the time Bodie reached town. He made his way along the street in the fading light until he was across from the squat building where Deeks had his office. Bodie paused to check the scattergun he'd picked up after the gunfight with the Jelks brothers. He'd found extra shells for the gun in Simm Jelks' pocket. Satisfied that the deadly shotgun was fully loaded and cocked, Bodie turned his attention to the building across the street.

"Deeks! It's Bodie! I left your boys out yonder for you to bury! But you got to go through me to get to 'em! If you got the guts, you son of a bitch!"

There was no response. Slowly Bodie began to cross the street, his eyes raking the frontage of the building.

"Come on out, Deeks! I heard you

had a big reputation in this town! Hard and mean, that's what they told me! They were wrong, Deeks! You ain't hard and you ain't mean! You're no better than a bag of horseshit! Deeks, you come out, or I'll drag you out!"

He had reached the middle of the street. Above him, at one of the upper windows, a figure moved, edging round so that he could push the barrel of a rifle through the bars. Bodie watched the moving barrel line upon him. He had the scattergun in the crook of his left arm, leaving his right hand free. Now he dropped the hand to the butt of his Colt, bringing it up in a smooth, easy action. The hammer was already back as the muzzle tilted up. Bodie eased back on the trigger. The Colt rapped out a single shot. The exposed barrel tilted skywards, the shadowy figure falling back inside the room.

Movement at the door drew Bodie's attention. He thrust the Colt away and swung the scattergun across to his right hand, finger resting on the triggers.

Three figures burst out through the door. Bodie recognised two of the men who had been in the office with Deeks the day he had arrived in High Grade. The third man was Deeks himself.

Bodie triggered the scattergun's first barrel. The charge caught the closest man in the left hip, splintering the bone and ripping flesh apart. The man gave a terrified scream as the force of the charge lifted him, hurling him back across the boardwalk . . . and Deeks himself, halting in mid-stride, his hand lifting, levelling the gun he carried, firing . . . the bullet kicked up dirt inches to one side of Bodie . . . he turned sideways on, presenting a slimmer target, hearing the heavy blast of sound as he triggered the second barrel of the scattergun, felt the recoil of the weapon . . . and Deeks caught the full force of the charge in the face. A high, terrible scream of agony filled the air, and Deeks began to stumble blindly about, raising his hand to cover the awful mask of pulped flesh that had been his face; there was no feature left to be recognisable: it was as if Deeks' face had been wiped away, leaving behind a raw, bloody mass of pulsing flesh and splintered bone. Bodie tossed aside the scattergun and took out his Colt, lifting it, he fired twice, the bullets driving Deeks to the bloody ground.

"I'm out of it, Bodie!" the third man yelled. He threw his gun down on the ground and lifted his hands.

Bodie turned in his direction, his Colt exploding with noise. The man twisted violently, blood spurting from the ragged wound in his chest. He sprawled full length in the dust, one leg kicking awkwardly against approaching death.

"You are now, feller," Bodie said, and walked on by him, into the building.

He stood in the empty lobby, thumbing fresh loads into the Colt, waiting.

After a long time he heard a cautious footstep from somewhere in Deeks' office. A cold smile edged Bodie's mouth. He moved silently to the door and glanced into the room.

Jonas Randall stood in the very centre of the big office. He had a rifle gripped in his hands and he was staring in Bodie's direction.

"Bodie, can we talk?" he asked. There was a slight edge to his voice. Sweat gleamed on his face.

"Can't be done, feller," Bodie said.

"For God's sake why, Bodie?"

"It's a one-way conversation."

Randall frowned. "What is?"

"Talking to a dead man," Bodie explained.

Realisation hit Randall in that final moment. In desperation he jerked up the rifle he was holding. But he was too slow. Bodie put three bullets in him where he stood, the impact driving Randall back across the office. He struck the edge of Deeks' big desk, slithered along the polished top and struck the floor on his face. The back of his dark coat was wet with blood from the three fist-sized exit holes made by Bodie's bullets. Slick runnels of blood began to creep out from under his prone body.

"They keep saying conversation's a dying art, anyhow, feller," Bodie said.

He walked outside. Oddly he was now aware of a steady pulse of pain down his side where he'd caught some of the shot from Simm Jelks' scattergun. Putting his hand there he felt the swelling edges of the wound and the sticky warmth of blood. He pushed his way through the gathering crowd and began to walk up towards the Crown house at the top of the hill. It began to look a long, long way off, and he wondered if he'd make it.

Even in the gathering twilight he recognised Angela Crown's figure as she came down the hill. When she realised it was him she ran to him, staring at his bloody side.

"I heard the shooting," she said.

"Somehow I just knew it had to be you."

Bodie shrugged. "It's been that kind of a day."

"Bodie, what happened?"

"Let's just say Randall's withdrawn his offer for your mine. Permanently!"

Angela shook her head slowly. "You mean it's over?"

"That part is. But there's going to be one hell of a fuss when the law gets to hear what's been happening in High Grade."

Angela slipped her arm around his waist as they walked on up the hill. "Will you stay and help, Bodie? I think I need you."

"I walked into this mess with my eyes open," Bodie said. "I might as well go the course. I got a couple of good reasons to keep me here for a while."

Angela glanced at him, her face flushing warmly. "Oh?"

"Hell, yes. It's going to take some figuring out what bounty money I got coming from those gunslingers Randall had on his payroll. With my luck the law'll contest every claim I make! I could be there for weeks!"

"What's the other reason?" Angela asked hopefully.

"Kind of embarrassing," Bodie said. "See, we never did get round to talking money after you hired me to ride shotgun on that wagon you brought in. Things kind of got a little busy after we got here."

"Bodie, I hope you choke on every cent," Angela said.

"Way I see it, a deal's a deal!" He thought for a moment. "Mind, we could make some kind of arrangement."

"Oh? What did you have in mind?"

"Kind of a more personal sort of payment," Bodie suggested.

A slow smile spread across Angela's face. "Sounds interesting, Mr Bodie. I'm sure we could reach an satisfactory conclusion."

"Damn right we could, Miss Crown."

"And I do believe I could come up

with an offer later tonight."

"Yeah?"

As they reached the house and Angela pushed open the door, she turned to glance at him, pink tongue drifting lightly across her soft lips. "Most definitely. And I even think there might be a bonus or two in it for you!"

Bodie followed her inside. He was thinking it might be worth considering investing some of his money in Crown mine stock. The way Angela played the game, collecting his dividends could take on a whole new meaning.

Other titles in the
Linford Western Library:

TOP HAND
Wade Everett

The Broken T was big. But no ranch is big enough to let a man hide from himself.

GUN WOLVES OF LOBO BASIN
Lee Floren

The Feud was a blood debt. When Smoke Talbot found the outlaws who gunned down his folks he aimed to nail their hide to the barn door.

SHOTGUN SHARKEY
Marshall Grover

The westbound coach carrying the indomitable Larry and Stretch headed for a shooting showdown.

FIGHTING RAMROD
Charles N. Heckelmann

Most men would have cut their losses, but Frazer counted the bullets in his guns and said he'd soak the range in blood before he'd give up another inch of what was his.

LONE GUN
Eric Allen

Smoke Blackbird had been away too long. The Lequires had seized the Blackbird farm, forcing the Indians and settlers off, and no one seemed willing to fight! He had to fight alone.

THE THIRD RIDER
Barry Cord

Mel Rawlins wasn't going to let anything stand in his way. His father was murdered, his two brothers gone. Now Mel rode for vengeance.

ARIZONA DRIFTERS
W. C. Tuttle

When drifting Dutton and Lonnie Steelman decide to become partners they find that they have a common enemy in the formidable Thurston brothers.

TOMBSTONE
Matt Braun

Wells Fargo paid Luke Starbuck to outgun the silver-thieving stagecoach gang at Tombstone. Before long Luke can see the only thing bearing fruit in this eldorado will be the gallows tree.

HIGH BORDER RIDERS
Lee Floren

Buckshot McKee and Tortilla Joe cut the trail of a border tough who was running Mexican beef into Texas. They stopped the smuggler in his tracks.

BRETT RANDALL, GAMBLER
E. B. Mann

Larry Day had the choice of running away from the law or of assuming a dead man's place. No matter what he decided he was bound to end up dead.

THE GUNSHARP
William R. Cox

The Eggerleys weren't very smart. They trained their sights on Will Carney and Arizona's biggest blood bath began.

THE DEPUTY OF SAN RIANO
Lawrence A. Keating and Al. P. Nelson

When a man fell dead from his horse, Ed Grant was spotted riding away from the scene. The deputy sheriff rode out after him and came up against everything from gunfire to dynamite.

FARGO: MASSACRE RIVEI
John Benteen

The ambushers up ahead had no
blocked the road. Fargo's conv
was a jumble, a perfect target
the insurgents' weapons!

SUNDANCE: DEATH IN TI
LAVA
John Benteen

The Modoc's captured the wag
train and its cargo of gold. But n
the halfbreed they called Sundar
was going after it . . .

HARSH RECKONING
Phil Ketchum

Five years of keeping himself al
in a brutal prison had made Bra
tough and careless about who
gunned down . . .

AMERICAN ANIMALS

PAINTINGS BY
AUDUBON

EDITED BY
DORIS R. MILLER

THE MULBERRY PRESS, INC. • NEW YORK

SBN 0-88302-362-8

TABLE OF CONTENTS

MOUNTAIN GOAT

THE mountain goat makes his home among the high mountain rocks. In winter, he comes down to look for grass to eat. Mountain goats often weigh up to 300 pounds.

AMERICAN BISON

THE bison is also called the buffalo. He is one of the largest animals in America. Hunters have killed so many of them that there are very few bison left in the United States today.

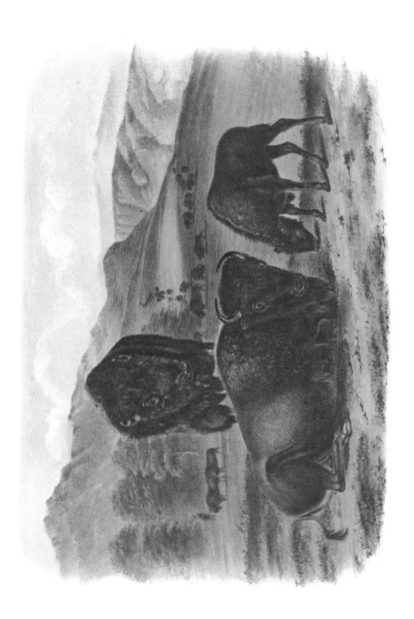

PRONGHORN

THE pronghorn can run very fast. He lives on the plains or in the desert. The pronghorn has very sharp eyes. He can see for many miles.

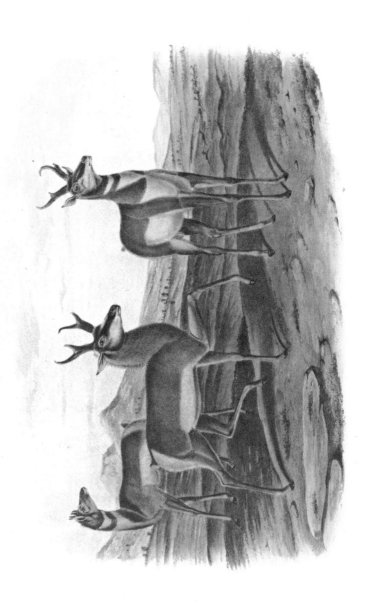

DEER

WHITE-TAILED deer live everywhere in the United States. They are protected by law. Deer feed on leaves, twigs, and fruit. They are about four feet tall and nearly seven feet long.

MOOSE

THE moose is the largest of all American deer. He can grow as large as seven feet high. He can be very dangerous. Even bears get out of his way. The moose eats lilies and other plants that grow in water.

COLLARED PECCARY

THE collared peccary is a wild pig. He eats worms, nuts, plants, and snakes. He has strong, sharp hooves, which he uses to kill rattlesnakes.

COUGAR

THE cougar is the biggest cat in the United States. He is very strong. A cougar can kill a big deer. He will hunt for many miles without any rest.

OTTER

OTTERS build their homes near streams and rivers. They eat fish, frogs, and turtles. They are playful and like to swim.

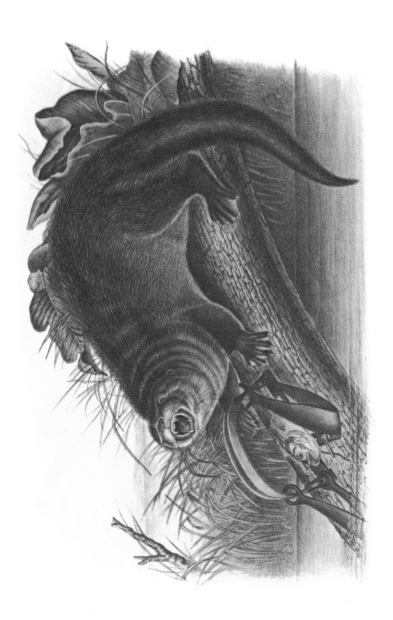

MINK

THE mink can live on land or in the water. On land he hunts rabbits to eat. When he is in the water, he eats fish and frogs. His fur is valuable for women's coats.

LONG-TAILED WEASEL

THE long-tailed weasel is brave and fierce. He likes to hunt at night. He eats mice, rats, and birds. He changes color with the seasons, becoming white in winter and brown in summer.

ESKIMO DOG

THE Eskimo dogs pull sleds over the ice and snow. They are also used for hunting polar bears. The Eskimo dog doesn't bark. He howls, just like a wolf.

BLACK BEAR

SOMETIMES the black bear can be a friend. Then he is a lot of fun. But he can also hurt people. He can climb trees and he can swim. The black bear eats fish and honey.

COYOTE

THE coyote is also called the prairie wolf. He hunts and eats rabbits and rats. In this way he helps the farmer.

RED FOX

THE red fox is full of tricks. He is hard to catch. At night he curls up on the ground to sleep.

SWIFT FOX

SWIFT foxes can run very fast, but they are easy to hunt and trap. A swift fox comes out to hunt for food only at night. He eats insects, mice, and snakes.

PORCUPINE

PORCUPINES mainly live in forests. The porcupine is covered with almost 30,000 quills. Stay away from him! His quills are sharp and stick in whatever touches them.

BLACK-TAILED
PRAIRIE DOG

THE prairie dog really belongs to the squirrel family. But he barks like a dog. When danger is near, the prairie dog whistles to warn his friends.

WOODCHUCK

THE woodchuck eats and eats in the summer. Then he stays in his den all winter. He digs his den under an open field. The woodchuck is also called the groundhog.

WOOD RAT

THE wood rat likes to come out at night. He steals and hides anything he can carry. He runs along the branches of trees like a squirrel.

HUDSON'S BAY LEMMING

LEMMINGS are about 6 inches long. They look like rats. They change color from one season to another. In the winter they are white, and in the summer they are brown. Lemmings eat grass and roots.

FOX SQUIRREL

THE fox squirrel does not run very fast. He lives on the edge of the forest. Here he finds his food. He likes nuts, fruit, and seeds.

FLYING SQUIRREL

FLYING squirrels do not really fly. They glide through the air from one tree limb to another. They sleep all day and hunt for food at night.

BLACK-TAILED RABBIT

THE black-tailed rabbit lives in the open country. He runs very fast and is hard to catch. Farmers don't like him because he eats the vegetables in their gardens.

SNOWSHOE RABBIT

THE snowshoe rabbit has large feet covered with long fur. They help him to travel over ice and snow. That is why he is called the snowshoe rabbit.

MOLE

A MOLE spends his life under the ground. He must dig all the time to get the food he needs. He uses his heavy claws to dig for insects, beetles, and angleworms.

OPOSSUM

WHEN an opossum is frightened, he plays "dead." He lies on the ground all curled up. He lies very, very still. When a person is very still or makes believe he is asleep, we say, "He is playing 'possum'."

SKUNK

SKUNKS help farmers everywhere. They eat harmful insects, grubs, and small animals. They give off a bad smell only when they are frightened. But you should not get too close to a skunk!

GRAY WOLF

GRAY wolves grow to be seven feet long. They usually weigh about 150 pounds. Long ago, the gray wolf lived in many parts of the country. Today, it is hard to find a gray wolf in the United States. He is found mostly in Canada.

BADGER

You can tell a badger by the white stripe that runs from his nose to the back of his head. Badgers are small animals. They have strong, long teeth and claws. They live in dens, which they dig for themselves.

JOHN JAMES AUDUBON

JOHN JAMES AUDUBON was born in Santo Domingo, in 1785. When Audubon was very young, his father took him to Paris. There he studied with the great French painter Jacques Louis David. This was the only training that Audubon ever got as an artist.

When he was seventeen, Audubon came to the United States. Audubon spent most of his life painting birds and animals. In 1838 he published his *Birds of America.* People from all over the world praised his beautiful paintings.

Audubon was finishing his book of paintings of the animals of North America when he died in 1851. His sons finished the work.

The Audubon Society is named after this great painter and naturalist.

Other Books You Will Enjoy

For information, write: The Mulberry Press, Inc.
845 Third Avenue
New York, New York 10022